Divided Loyalties

Outlaw gang leader Curly Ben Clovis has heard about shipments of silver being stored at the town of Hashknife in southern Colorado. Shot and badly wounded in a failed holdup, Clovis sends his lieutenant, Jim Kane, to suss out the best way of seizing the valuable haul once he has recovered.

Kane is mistaken for the new lawman and quickly calculates that assuming the guise of Marshal Jonas Kelly will put him in a more favourable position to organise the proposed robbery. Little does the outlaw realize the quandary in which he will become embroiled and he is forced to make choices, the outcome of which will lead to double dealing and bloodshed.

Divided Loyalties

Ethan Flagg

A Black Horse Western

ROBERT HALE · LONDON

© Ethan Flagg 2008
First published in Great Britain 2008

ISBN 978-0-7090-8671-0

Robert Hale Limited
Clerkenwell House
Clerkenwell Green
London EC1R 0HT

www.halebooks.com

Typeset by
Derek Doyle & Associates, Shaw Heath
Printed and bound in Great Britain by
CPI Antony Rowe, Wiltshire

ONE

HOLD-UP!

Vic Bodie flipped up the cover of his gold pocket watch.

It read 2.17 p.m.

The timepiece was a treasured possession that had been procured from a wealthy banker. The man had been none too pleased at having the prized bauble forcibly removed from his person. A bleeding skull courtesy of Vic's Remington Rider had encouraged the blustering stagecoach passenger to relinquish ownership in double-quick time.

That had been during a hold-up the gang had successfully undertaken along this route the previous month.

And here they were again, secreted behind a cluster of boulders in the very same spot. Much against the considered opinion of his doughty lieutenant, Curly Ben Clovis had insisted on it.

'Stands to reason, Vic,' the gang leader had stressed, a touch irritated at having his authority put into question. 'The haulage company won't be expecting another heist along the same route so soon after the last one. They'll figure we wouldn't be that stupid.' Clovis grinned. It emerged more in the way of a twisted grimace. 'Well, they hadn't bargained on coming up against Curly Ben Clovis.' The gang leader arrogantly rolled his eyes.

Bodie was not convinced, but he felt it wise not to press the issue. You could only push Curly Ben so far before he let that new .45 cartridge revolver do the persuading. Wolfie Krebbs had learned the hard way. And they had buried him on the side of the trail.

So here they were, second time around.

Jim Kane likewise had his fingers crossed hoping that the boss's theory was sound. The other members of the gang were ranged on either side of the narrow ravine known as Manzanola Draw. It was the only feasible route through which the Silverton trail could pass.

As on previous occasions, they were all keyed up, tense and expectant, not quite knowing if things would go according to plan. A cocky young hard ass calling himself the Dakota Kid was puffing nervously on a cheroot.

'Put that blasted thing out,' hollered Clovis, spearing the Kid with the evil eye. 'D'yuh wanna give our position away?'

The Kid's lip twisted, a peevish frown darkening his youthful features. But he remained silent, and the quirly was extinguished.

'D'yuh reckon the stage is on time?' Bodie asked, wiping the sweat from his brow. There was no shade from the hot sun which beat down remorselessly from a cloudless azure sky. He stuck the watch face to his ear, listening to make sure it was working.

Clovis emitted a sigh of exasperation.

'Goldarn it, Vic,' he snapped. 'That's the third time you've asked me that. And I'll give you the same goddamn answer. It always leaves Silverton at ten-thirty in the morning. And with no hold-ups. . . .'

A rumbling chortle erupted from between the thick lips of Bulldog Maddox. 'That's a good one, boss,' guffawed the heavy-set bruiser. 'No hold-ups!'

But Clovis was in no mood for hilarity. An acerbic growl rolled around his tight-jawed mouth. Lowering black eyes arrowed the fatuous tough as the withering look quickly snuffed out the varmint's attempt at levity.

'As I was saying' – the delivery was granite-edged – 'if nothing goes wrong, it should take around four hours to reach Manzanola Draw.'

Ben Clovis checked his own timepiece.

A curt nod set the thick mass of dark curls swaying beneath his black Stetson. It oughta be here just about now.

'Check your hardware, boys,' he ordered, while casually spinning the chamber of his nickel-plated Peacemaker. The pistol was not yet on the open market being available only to officers of the law. The owner had been leading a posse that had got too close during a chase out of Tucumcari. Once the lawdog

7

had bitten the dust, thanks to the unerring aim of Jim Kane's Henry, the posse members had quickly got the message and turned back empty-handed.

Bodie eyed the weapon enviously. He fully intended to acquire his own .45 after this job, and with carved ivory grips too.

A ratcheting of pistol cylinders blended with the heavier clump of rifle levers being cranked. Harshly metallic, the ominous sound of imminent combat echoed between the narrow walls of the draw.

'Me and Vic will make the first move, the same as we did afore,' Clovis reminded his men. With one accord they nodded empathically. 'Soon as we've gotten the stage driver to haul rein, you boys make your presence known, just to encourage them not to try any fancy stuff.' Curly Ben allowed himself a wry smirk which was taken up by the rest of the gang. Then just as quickly, he reverted back to a serious vein adding, 'And keep your eyes peeled. Any sly manoeuvres, you let 'em have it. Savvy?'

At that moment, the lumbering rumble of the stage-coach could be heard in the distance. Swirling skeins of yellow dust spiralled above a clump of dessicated juniper heralding its impending arrival. A buzzard cawed overhead, its lazy search for a late lunch disturbed by these human interlopers.

Keen eyes peered along rifle barrels as the men waited expectantly. Clovis quickly scanned the environs of the tapering draw to make certain his men were in position.

Bulldog Maddox stood out like a sore thumb, his

lumpy features topped by the large Texas Sugarloaf announcing his presence to all the world. Clovis grunted with exasperation. Did these turkeys never learn? Immediately, he signalled for the hulking outlaw to remove his hat and find a more prudent site below the rimrock.

Maddox returned the urgent gesture with a look of bewilderment before realizing what was expected. He raised an arm in acknowledgement then disappeared from view. In stark contrast, Jim Kane knew instinctively where the optimum place of concealment was to be found. Clovis afforded him barely a glance. Why couldn't he find more guys like Kane?

The Kid was an unknown quantity. Dakota had only joined them a couple of weeks before and this was his first job. There were no doubts in Curly Ben's devious mind that his prowess with a sixgun was clear. Indeed, the Kid was probably the fastest draw in the gang. Even Vic Bodie would be no match for him in a straight shoot out.

Only Chavez was absent.

After the last job, the Mexican had left for his home town of Shiprock over the border in New Mexico. He had received a wire that his father had been shot, apparently by a cavalry sergeant who hated greasers.

Clovis shrugged. The Mex was second to none up close with a knife, but his long range shooting left much to be desired.

Just then, the stagecoach clattered round a bend at the far end of the draw, a billowing trail of dust in its wake.

Clovis smiled. Only one guy on top. They hadn't even bothered to employ a guard. This was gonna be easy as stealing whiskey from a blind man.

It was a quarter-mile from the entrance of Manzanola Draw to where the gang was secreted. The atmosphere crackled with suppressed tension. It was always the same before a hold-up.

At one hundred yards, the constricted nature of the trail forced the stage driver to slow the team of six to a gentle trot. Before he could whip them up again, Ben with Vic Bodie at his side rode out blocking the way forward.

Both had their six-shooters raised and cocked.

'Rein up, driver, this is a hold-up,' hollered Clovis, waving the gun with menacing intent. 'Don't make no fancy moves and you won't get hurt. All we want is the strong box under your seat.'

'You heard the man,' stressed Bodie while nudging his sorrel forward. 'And be damned quick about it.'

Initially, the driver appeared to have been taken by surprise. His mouth gaped wide. Automatically he dragged on the reins bringing the team down to a walk.

Then it happened.

'Yaaaahooo!'

The high-pitched halloo echoed back from the enclosed rocky enclave as the driver whipped up the horses. Bent low, he continued yelling as the coach quickly gathered speed. 'OK, you crazy cayuses, let's show these varmints what we're made of.'

That was the signal for all hell to break loose.

10

Gun barrels immediately poked through the coach's open windows.

'Let 'em have it, boys!' shouted a fired-up voice from within. 'And remember there's a bonus if we get this shipment through to Durango intact.'

A fusillade of shots followed, white smoke and flame belching forth in rapid fire. On the roof of the coach, a luggage tarpaulin was thrust aside as two more heads appeared, their guns opening up on the confounded road agents.

Bodie was killed outright, punched off the back of his horse by a half-dozen accurately placed rifle bullets.

Ever the professional gunman, Clovis quickly recovered. Ducking low behind his mount's neck he cut loose with his six-shooter. But his aim was wildly inaccurate. As the coach passed by in a flurry of smoke and dust, he let fly with his second pistol into the open window. Somebody must have been hit judging from the discordant yelp of pain that assailed the gang-leader's ringing ears.

But it was all too much. Clovis stood no chance against such a display of firepower. He swayed ungainly like a rag doll as a bullet ploughed into his chest. Another drilled through soft thigh muscle burying itself in his mount. The animal reared up before tumbling to the ground. Luckily, Clovis was thrown clear of the thrashing hoofs.

Only then did the rest of the gang retaliate.

Skittish and edgy, the Kid was first to react. Leaping to his feet, he emptied the full magazine of his Henry repeater into the coach. But his feckless bravado was no match for the concealed guards. A cry of anguish spewed from his twisted mouth as he went down.

The coach rattled away along the draw, soon hidden from view under the welter of dust. Maddox and Kane blindly propelled a storm of shells after the retreating coach, but to no avail. All they received in response was an exuberant cheer from the coach guardians who were clearly flushed by the successful defence of the silver shipment.

It was Jim Kane who called a halt to the pointless waste of ammunition.

With one man dead, the Kid out of action and their leader writhing in agony on the ground, there was no chance of regrouping and heading off in pursuit. In fact, unless they lit out pronto and made themselves scarce, there was every chance that the defenders could return and finish the job.

It was late evening before the sorry group of riders reached their bolthole in the San Juan Mountains. It had been a tough journey. Bodie had been left for the buzzards to feed on. Jim Kane had more pressing concerns for the welfare of the living.

Clovis was in a bad way. He was losing a lot of blood. Having to ride double behind Kane hadn't helped. Apart from a makeshift bandage, nothing more could be done for the gang leader until they reached Mineral Springs.

Spectral fingers of approaching night crept over the open glade below Conejos Peak where the cabin

12

was located, smothering the harsh terrain with a dark mantle of shadow. Gathering clouds had blotted out the moon's weak light heralding the imminent approach of rain.

The log cabin backed on to a soaring overhang of rock. It had once been home to a couple of silver miners. But they had long since abandoned the claim when the pay dirt had run out. It now played host to Curly Ben Clovis and his gang, though the sorry-looking misfits now stumbling into the cabin bore no visible resemblance to the self-assured bunch who had left before daybreak that morning.

Kane quickly took control. He ordered Bulldog Maddox to build a fire and boil up some water. The heavy bruiser was too stupefied to demur and set about the alloted task in a daze.

There were bullets to be removed and wounds to be cleaned.

The Kid's injury was only superficial and could wait. He sat in a corner hunched over a half-empty bottle of rye whiskey muttering to himself.

Kane reasoned that unless he got that slug out of Curly Ben soon, the gang leader would surely peg out.

With a brutal ten-inch Bowie gripped tightly in his fist, Kane wrenched the bottle from the Kid's reluctant grasp and offered it to Curly Ben Clovis. The gang leader imbibed deeply.

'This is gonna hurt you—'

Clovis interrupted him with a hard grin whilst attempting to hold his sidekick's steady gaze. His eyes were red-rimmed and yellow. 'Yeah! I know,' he croaked. 'It's gonna hurt me a sight more'n it hurts you.' He emitted a throaty glug. The effort at hilarity precipitated a howl of pain. 'Don't make me laugh, Jim boy.' Clovis coughed up a globule of bright red. 'It hurts too damn much. Just dig the bastard out.'

'Here, boss.' Maddox had managed to shrug off his previous lethargic torpor and now handed his leader a leather belt. 'It'll help some if'n yuh bite down hard.'

Clovis nodded his thanks.

'Let's get it over with then,' he wheezed, screwing up his weather-beaten face in readiness.

Kane poured a liberal dose of hard liquor over the ragged bullet hole, took a deep breath, and went to work.

TWO

CHAVEZ RETURNS

Kane was grateful that the initial probing had caused Ben Clovis to lose consciousness. It made his job all the easier. Even so, the elusive bullet took some finding. Eventually, however, after much delving it flipped out, an ugly chunk of lead. At a nod from Kane, Maddox handed him a poker that had been heating in the fire. This was the part of the operation where Kane was glad that his patient was still out cold.

The end glowed red hot.

'Hold him down,' Kane ordered the burly tough firmly. 'Just in case.'

Maddox complied, his sagging jowls ashen. His sweaty mug glistened in the harsh light cast by the livid poker. Even hardcases like him were apt to pale when confronted with this most grisly of medical tasks.

Kane hesitated momentarily. A look of solid determination passed between the pair of outlaws. Then he jabbed the gleaming tip into the torn flesh surrounding the gunshot wound. The soft flesh sizzled and hissed as the edges cauterized, the sickly odour of roasting meat clawing at their throats. It was all the more repellant knowing it was from a human source.

But sealing the wound was vital to protect against infection. And, thankfully, Curly Ben remained oblivious of the brutal torture to which his body was being subjected. The leg wound was child's play in comparison, requiring only a clean-up and bandaging as the bullet had gone right through.

'Yuh reckon he'll make it?' drawled an anxious Bulldog Maddox whilst worriedly eyeing the comatose body. Not the brightest button in the box, he was a follower who needed someone to give him a lead, tell him what to do. For the last four years, that guy had followed Curly Ben Clovis. And Maddox had grown used to the gang boss's waspish temperament.

Kane wiped the blood from his hands and took a hefty swig of the hard liquor before answering. 'We'll only know that if he regains consciousness.'

'And when will that be?'

A weary shrug accompanied Kane's reply. 'Two, maybe three days.'

In fact it was a week before Curly Ben rejoined the land of the living. He was extremely weak. His greying moustache hung limp beneath the beaky nose, the gaunt features blanched and pallid following the ordeal that he was more than gratified to have missed.

Thankfully, the worst was now over. Fever had not

set in and the wound was beginning to heal. And he was more than willing to wolf down a double helping of Maddox's rabbit stew. Nevertheless, Clovis was the first to appreciate that he would still be out of action for at least a month.

But that didn't stop him from planning the gang's next job, especially following the disastrous attempt at robbing the Silverton stage.

Clovis felt that his reputation was on the line. After all, it was he who had insisted they repeat the successful formula from the previous month. He realized too late that he should have heeded the cautionary warning from Bodie. The mining company had well and truly caught him out.

His lieutenant was dead, and the gang was becoming restive, uneasy. Dakota in particular had been heard to voice his concerns to Bulldog Maddox. Only Kane appeared unwilling to apportion blame in his direction for the calamitous setback.

For that, Clovis was much obliged. He had come to appreciate that Jim Kane was a steady and reliable hand with a sharp brain. He would make a first-rate henchman.

Clovis made the offer one afternoon when the other two were out hunting.

'I want you to be my second-in-command,' he proposed, while chewing on a burnt rabbit leg. He was propped up on a bunk in the back room of the cabin. 'Now that Bodie's hit the high road, I need someone I can trust. Someone who'll back me up when things get hairy. I reckon you fit the bill. What d'yuh say?'

Kane had been changing the bandages.

He surveyed his boss with a chary eye. Curly Ben's nonchalant mien gave nothing away. But he appeared to be serious.

'Naturally,' continued the gang boss breezily, 'you'll be given a bigger cut from all future jobs.'

Again he waited, expectantly.

Kane was tempted. He rolled a stogie, lit up and strolled round the room. Blank and expressionless, his close-set features gave nothing away. More dough at the payoff sounded good. But how would it fare with the others?

He smiled inwardly at the notion of Bulldog Maddox in such a position. And the Kid was an unknown quantity. Only the the Mexican presented a problem. He had been with Clovis from the start and might expect some reward for that.

And if he refused the offer? A bullet in the back from the Kid, or an unwelcome introduction to Chavez' knife, although he was confident of being able to handle any dissent.

Turning back to face Clovis he held out his hand. 'OK, boss, you got yourself a deal.'

For the first time in a week, Curly Ben's angular features cracked in a genuine smile. It was a rare sight.

'Let's drink on it,' he grinned.

Before they could even raise their glasses, the ominous clatter of pounding hoofs outside the cabin assailed their ears. Kane stiffened, his hand automatically reaching for the holstered Army Remington on his hip. The smile slipped from Curly Ben's face as his thick eyebrows knitted into a disquieting regard. All thoughts of celebration rapidly evaporated.

'Go see who that is!'

The order was brusque and forceful.

Kane left the back room in time to see the small Mexican hustling into the shack. His clothes were caked in dust indicating that he had ridden hard.

'Where boss?' he called out, panic evident in the rising cadence of the lilting accent. 'I hear in Durango that hold-up go badly. Mine guards brag they shoot up gang.'

'Easy there, *amigo.*' Kane's composed tones were meant to calm the ruffled Mexican. 'The boss is OK, just a slight graze, is all. The Kid was also shot but it was only a flesh wound.'

'Where Bodie?'

'Feedin' the buzzards.'

A fractured voice from the back room silenced further questioning.

'In here, Chavez.'

When the Mexican entered the room, he was stunned by the severity of the gang leader's injury. But Clovis shrugged off his concerns. He had other more important issues to discuss.

'So did you find anything out in Hashknife?' he pressed, levering himself up on one elbow and grabbing the little man's arm. 'Was it as I figured?'

Chavez nodded urgently.

'New mine opened in Trujillo Canyon. Silver being shipped through Hashknife.'

'Anything else?' Clovis scowled. He was expecting a

full-blown account. 'You were supposed to sniff out the whole caboodle so's I could plan a raid that would set us all up for life. What happened?'

The Mexican looked crestfallen. His shoulders lifted in a languid gesture of uncertainty.

'Once Father's shooting avenged, I leave Shiprock pretty damn quick with flea in ear. Army not like Chavez gutting their own man.' A rabid growl issued from between Clovis's pursed lips. The singsong delivery was grating on his nerves. He did not want to hear this. But Chavez carried on undeterred. 'Bluebellies chase poor self all way across Animas Plateau. Thought I had given slip, but like stubborn bloodhound, they kept on tail.'

'You didn't bring 'em here, did yuh?' Clovis growled acidly. His right hand was ominously fingering the butt of his prized Colt .45.

'No! No!' exclaimed the Mexican vehemently shaking his bullet head. 'Lost them in Bonanza Badlands. But had to leave Hashknife in hurry. No chance learn all about silver.'

Clovis frowned. 'This changes things.' Turning to Kane he snapped, 'Give me a drink. I need to think this out.'

Once the gang leader had secured the bottle, a casual wave of the arm dismissed the two men who then retreated to the main room.

It was late in the day before Clovis emerged from the back room. He hobbled painfully across the dirt floor and slumped into a chair.

'How yuh feelin', boss?' enquired Maddox, hand-

20

ing Clovis a steaming mug of coffee.

'How d'yuh think?' snapped Curly Ben, tipping a hefty slug of whiskey into the brew. He took a long slurp. 'That's better,' he sighed. Then without further preamble began to outline his thoughts on how the gang were going to relieve the Trujillo Mine of its rich bounty.

But without more information there was nothing he could do. A flinty eye focused on Jim Kane.

'You're gonna have to go to Hashknife and suss out the place,' he said. 'Figure out all the angles – shipments, protection, routes, that sort of thing.' From beneath hooded brows drawn tight with concentration, Clovis studied his new lieutenant closely searching for any sign of hesitancy or unease. 'Reckon you're up to it?'

Kane returned the boss's rigid stare with an equal measure of stolidity.

'When do you want me to leave?' he replied, tersely.

Clovis smiled. His judgement regarding Kane had been on the ball.

'First light,' he said. 'Shouldn't take you more'n three days hard ridin' to reach Hashknife. Book yourself into a hotel. And keep yer head down.' Clovis laid emphasis on his final remark as he handed over a wad of greenbacks for expenses. 'Last thing I need is you drawin' attention from a nosy tinstar.'

Kane drew himself up. 'I ain't no greenhorn, Ben,' he rapped back. 'You should know that.'

'Just make sure to have things sewn up tight as a banker's fist when me and the boys arrive in

21

Hashknife.' The brittle retort was meant to consolidate his authority as gang leader. Kane allowed himself a brief smile acknowledging the gesture with a curt nod of the head.

'When d'yuh figure that to be?' he asked.

Curly Ben's thick eyebrows lifted in thought. 'I reckon four weeks should see us linkin' up.'

The false dawn had daubed a trace of ochre across the eastern skyline when Jim Kane left Mineral Springs. His saddle-bags were packed tight with enough supplies for a four-day trek. Close by, a tawny owl hooted as it searched for an early breakfast. The only other sound to disturb the crisp morning air was the raucous snoring of his sidekicks.

At a gentle trot, Kane nudged his mount away from the golden sun rising majestically above the distant San Juan Range. This was new country to Kane. He had never ventured further west than Cimmaron. Soon after midday he had reached the swirling waters of the Rio Grande at a point where the mighty river had cut a notch through a deep ravine. Forced to head north, he eventually reached a ferry crossing at Alamosa.

Thereafter according to the vague instructions passed on by Chavez, it was an easy trek direct to Hashknife. The Mexican had claimed the location of the town was discernible from afar due to its proximity to a surging mesa of orange rock known as Pueblo Bonita. But he had forgotten to mention the vast ponderosa pine forests in between where the trail disappeared altogether.

More than once Kane had to retrace his steps having lost his way.

It came as no surprise that after five days the outlaw's supplies were exhausted. His prowess with a rifle now came in useful for hunting wild game. Supplemented with hazelnuts and late blueberries, the roast antelope was a welcome change from greasy fatback and beans.

Eventually after a week on the trail, Pueblo Bonita hove into view.

Hashknife lay beyond the isolated tower of orange sandstone, barely discernible amidst the arid expanse of sagebrush and mesquite. Kane reined in his lathered cayuse, screwing his eyes against the sun's blistering glare.

'Can you see it, old gal?' he whispered into the sorrel mare's twitching right ear. The horse snickered, its proud head bobbing emphatically. Kane followed the direction, his grey eyes widening as he picked out the tiny collection of wooden buildings. 'Now ain't you the clever one,' he chirped, carefully kneeing the horse down a gradient of loose shale.

THREE

HASHKNIFE

While still a quarter-mile from the town limits of Hashknife, Kane was aware of people staring at this bizarre apparition heading in from the east. It was as if they had never had visitors before. He paused, rested his gloved hands on the saddle horn and cautiously surveyed the odd behaviour.

Two men stood in the middle of the dusty street shielding their eyes. Both parties eyed one another for a full minute before the duo suddenly turned about and raced off up the street. They disappeared into a clapboard structure on the right.

Kane sat there, unmoving, unsure as to how he should proceed. He scratched his ear, a mannerism that displayed the outlaw's confusion. Slowly he backed the sorrel towards a lone cottonwood, its splayed branches offering a modicum of protection should this suspicious behaviour result in gunplay.

24

The outlaw's grey eyes narrowed, then widened as a hint of understanding filtered through the grey fog of his deliberations.

Word of the calamitous hold-up must have reached this backwater. Maybe the town marshal had a Wanted dodger pinned up with the face of Jim Kane displayed for all to see. He speculated idly as to how much reward he merited. Without thinking, the Remington was palmed and the loading checked.

Even now as he sat undecided beneath the cotton-wood canopy, alien guns could be fanning out amid the bleak wilderness, striking a bead in his direction.

Had Kane been able to inspect himself as he approached the remote settlement, he would have observed a man set tall in the saddle. Broad shoulders filling out the fringed buckskin jacket emphasized a solid and resolute character. A wide-brimmed Stetson, edged with a rattlesnake hat band, surmounted the imposing figure. And the dusky outline appeared all the more impressive against the backdrop of scintillating blue.

Jim Kane was no ordinary desperado who had viewed the expanding western territories as an easy means of earning a quick buck. Hailing from wealthy Kentucky stock, his father had been a state senator before the war decimated the family inheritance.

Jonas Kelly as he was then, had stuck with family tradition by joining General Lee's army. But the boy's war had not gone well. Captured and imprisoned in the infamous Lynchburg Stockade, he had eventually escaped and joined the notorious hit-and-run gang led by William Clark Quantrill. And, just like his friends the James boys, Jonas had been forced into a life of crime following the South's humiliating surrender in 1865.

That was when he decided to change his name.

In stark contrast, his brother Mitchell had always leaned towards the abolitionist viewpoint. It had caused numerous arguments between the two brothers. It was no surprise therefore, when Mitch elected to serve with the Northern forces. Mitch had quickly risen through the ranks ending up a colonel in charge of the 21st Ohio Foot. He had been present at the final victory signing at Appomattox Courthouse. A natural consequence had been for Mitch to assume a major role in helping with reconstruction of the shattered country on the side of law and order.

Since that final acrimonious parting of the ways, the two brothers had never met up. On numerous occasions though they had come close.

As sheriff of Butler County in Missouri, Mitch had led a posse in pursuit of outlaws who had robbed the Poplar Bluffs bank. The gang had escaped capture by disappearing into the mountain fastness of the Ozarks. He could not have known that his brother Jonas had been an active participant.

Kane had decided that discretion was the better form of valour and was preparing to withdraw when he saw a group of men walking towards him. None of them was carrying a gun. Not a sidearm nor a rifle between the four of them. This was becoming more bizarre by the minute.

He gently nudged the horse out from behind the tree, the pistol cocked and ready should the need arise.

When the quartet had come to within ten yards of the tall rider, Kane raised his left hand. 'That's far enough, gents,' he ordered brusquely, arcing the sixgun as a warning. 'You fellas got something on your minds?'

One of the men stepped forward. A portly, round-faced little man doffed his silk derby while stroking a white handkerchief across his sweating visage. Dressed in a suit that was tight in all the wrong places, he addressed Kane in an obsequious manner.

'Welcome to Hashknife,' he bowed, the bulbous head bobbing like a pecking chicken. 'My name is Elmer Flockhart. I am the town mayor and these gentlemen' – he waved to the shuffling group behind – 'are members of the town council. We weren't expecting you until next month.' The little man paused expectantly.

Kane looked from one to the other, a blank expression clouding the craggy profile in shadow beneath the wide hat. He was glad of the blurred image he presented. His sharp brain quickly latched on to the assumption that these dudes had been expecting someone else. They had clearly mistaken him for that unknown individual.

Realizing that his lawless activities were not an issue to these men, Kane allowed his tense body to relax. This could prove an interesting situation if he played it right. The issue was determining who he was meant to be.

Pushing back his hat, Kane greeted the delegation with an exaggerated sweep of his thick blond locks.

'Glad to make your acquaintance, gentlemen,' he smiled, returning the fawning gesture. 'I made better time than expected.' Then, slipping the pistol back into its holster, he added with a terse chortle, 'Can't be too careful in my line of work.' He hoped that this remark would cover a multitude of situations.

'You're certainly right there, Mister. . . ?'

A cool gleam pulsated from Kane's narrowed gaze. So they didn't know the mystery man's name. Even better. But if he was to make the most of this singular occurrence, Jim Kane would need to lie doggo for a while.

'Kelly, sir,' he announced, with a blasé intonation that was accompanied by a broad grin. 'Jonas Kelly hailing out of Denver.'

Another man stepped forward offering his hand.

'Glad to have you with us, Marshal Kelly. And welcome to Hashknife. Cranford Jagger's the name,' stated the tall, lanky dude who bore a distinct resemblance to an ageing rooster. 'I am owner and proprietor of the town's bank. That's where the silver is kept until we have amassed enough for a delivery to Durango.'

Kane was barely able to suppress a derisive laugh. With the greatest effort he managed to maintain the fixed oily grin.

Now we are really getting somewhere, he mused, shaking the man's flaccid hand. It felt like a wet fish in his palm. It was a lawman whom the town worthies were expecting.

Welcome Marshal *Jonas Kelly*.

It sounded good. But the outlaw knew that he would have to be on his guard at all times. One slip of the tongue and the subterfuge would be exposed. It was to be hoped that the real lawdog did not arrive in Hashknife before the next silver shipment could be lifted.

Jonas Kelly had a month to determine the best means of achieving this end.

'And how often does the silver get moved?' he enquired, rather too quickly.

'About once a month,' replied the banker.

Another man then stepped forward.

'Let me show you the new office we have made available for your use, Marshal.' The speaker was a large heavy-set jigger sporting a thick black beard and wearing a leather apron. Bulging arms of hardened muscle informed Jonas that this had to be the town blacksmith. A deep resonant baritone matched the big man's appearance. 'I've included a couple of cells at the back forged from the toughest steel bar,' added Hank Rogers with a proud flourish.

Even with a mayor and council, Hashknife could hardly merit the distinction of being called a town. But if the silver became a regular feature of its *raison d'être*, that situation would rapidly change. Indeed it was already happening. New buildings were in the course of being erected along a roadway branching off at right angles to Main.

The fourth member of the reception committee

was a small, mousy dude boasting a wispy grey moustache. Faron Bentley was the local storekeeper.

'That's our new theatre,' he announced in lordly fashion, pointing to a half-finished structure. 'We intend to have the finest artistes in the land performing in Hashknife before long.'

A wry smirk strayed across the would-be marshal's granite features, which he quickly replaced with one of stoic approval.

With Hank Rogers in the lead the small conclave marched up the street with Jonas riding behind. Townsfolk lined the boardwalks on either side, their curiosity aroused by the arrival of the new lawman. He felt like a general come to survey his newly conquored domain.

It was an extraneous though somewhat intoxicating experience.

After being ushered into his new quarters, the councillors left Jonas to settle in.

He pinned on the shiny five-pointed marshal's badge, sat down in the swivel chair and planted his scuffed boots on the old roll-top desk. In the corner, someone had thoughtfully lit a fire in the potbellied cast-iron stove where a pot of coffee was brewing. An adjoining table contained a silver tray with cups and saucers, milk and a sugar bowl, all neatly presented on an embroidered cloth.

A couple of paintings adorned the walls, each depicting some fine examples of horse flesh.

The place appeared to have been given a woman's touch. No bad thing, Jonas muttered to himself.

After pouring himself a cup of coffee, Jonas removed his hat, leaned back in the chair and rested his hands behind his head. A contented sigh filtered from between an even set of teeth. He could easily get used to this. The council had offered him a decent remuneration with extra payments dependent on his performance in the job. Tired eyes drooped as the long ride from Mineral Springs slowly took control of his body.

His head sagged as the sandman beckoned.

But it was not to be.

The sleep urgently claiming his weary frame was abruptly thrust aside.

FOUR

JONAS KELLY, MARSHAL

The office door swung back on its hinges revealing a slim profile etched starkly against the sunlight. Jonas almost fell out of his chair.

'What in tarnation!' he ejaculated, his hand dropping to the holstered pistol. 'That you already, Ben?' The chair scraped back as the surprised incumbent struggled to draw his pistol.

'Easy there, Marshal,' chided a light catchy voice that clearly emanated from a female source. 'Ain't gonna shoot me, are yuh, before we even have time to get acquainted?' The cheerful giggle brought a red flush to the new lawman's normally rugged visage.

Jonas shook the sluggishness from his brain, suddenly realizing where he was. The girl hadn't noticed anything untoward pertaining to his utterance

32

of the gang leader's name. All the same, it could have been a nasty moment. The need to remain ever vigilent elbowed itself to the forefront of his thoughts.

Quickly holstering the drawn pistol, Jonas mumbled an apology.

He was not slow in perceiving that although the girl presented a tomboyish appearance being clad in tight jeans and a checkered work shirt, underneath she was definitely all woman. A figure rounded in all the right places was topped by flaxen hair that cascaded over narrow shoulders. Her smile illuminated an alabaster complexion, smoothly contoured and radiant.

'Hope you enjoyed the coffee,' she said stepping into the dim interior where Jonas could see that none of his assumptions regarding the girl's allure had been mistaken. She held out a tiny hand which was engulfed by Jonas's huge, roughened paw. 'Rachel Summers,' she declared. 'Me and my pa run a horse ranch alone the San Cristobal ten miles north of town.'

Jonas cast his eyes towards the wall pictures.

'These fellas from your stock?' he asked.

'Sure are,' confirmed the girl, hands firmly planted on a pair of well-rounded hips. 'I paint in my spare time. Hope you approve.' Her gently appraising regard was hypnotic in its intensity.

Jonas shuffled uneasily under the potent gaze, merely nodding his affirmation. Sensing the new marshal's embarrassment, Rachel poured herself a cup of coffee before continuing, 'I thought you might appreciate a few feminine touches about the place.'

She pointed to the red and white gingham curtains on the outside window. 'Made those myself as well.'

Jonas quickly recovered his composure.

Much as he welcomed this attention from the lovely Rachel Summers, his real purpose for being in Hashknife had to take priority. Especially considering the freakish circumstances in which he had become embroiled.

'Nice to have met you, Miss Summers,' he said rising to his feet. 'But as I'm new here, it's best that I get myself acquainted with the town and its routines.' He touched the brim of his hat and gently ushered her to the door. 'And much obliged for the extras. Makes a fella feel right at home.'

The new lawdog's loose smile brought a flush to the girl's velvet cheeks. Now it was her turn to be embarrassed.

'Be seein' you around then, Marshal,' she finished, setting her hat back atop the thick wavy tresses.

'You can bet on it, Miss Summers,' replied a breezy Jonas Kelly. And the name's Ji— Jonas, if'n you've a mind.'

In the nick of time he'd managed to avoid a possibly dangerous slip of the tongue. After all this time, reverting to his born name would take some getting used to. He gulped. This job was going to be a tougher proposition than he had expected.

Rachel Summers hadn't noticed.

'Sure thing . . . Jonas,' she grinned, green eyes fluttering coquettishly. 'Gotta get back to the ranch anyways. I allus help Pa with the branding at this time of year before we drive the horses down to Fort Sumner.'

Then she flounced off down the boardwalk, hips swaying provocatively. Whether or not it was a deliberate ploy, Jonas didn't care to speculate. He had other things on his mind.

And the first of these was to investigate the new silver mine and its operation. He sauntered across the street to make his presence known to the one guy in any town who knew everything.

Pushing open the door of the Silver Wheel Saloon, he entered the dim interior of the town's only drinking parlour. If the mine proved to be a regular and profitable venture, that would soon change as other such establishments sprang up to cater for the needs of a boom town economy.

Only a few drinkers were in residence. Two cowpunchers leaned on the bar that occupied the whole of the right wall. They were watching a poker game where the stakes were in silver nuggets. It appeared that already the mother lode was attracting other prospectors into the vicinity.

A swamper idly pushed a broom across the floor.

'Howdy, Marshal,' he said.

Jonas ignored the man's greeting as he peered around the room.

'It's a custom around here for a new marshal to buy a drink for the first guy who speaks to him,' pressed the swamper, upping his tone slightly. Even a lowly saloon hick likes to be acknowledged.

Still Jonas remained silent.

'Don't you he bothering the marshal, Soapy,' rapped Clancy the bartender. 'He ain't here to support the likes of you.'

Soapy Saunders cursed under his breath, then grudgingly turned away. Only then did Jonas realize that the guy had been addressing him.

Another mistake!

Quickly he extracted a coin from his vest pocket and called out to the retreating form of the indignant swamper.

'Hey, Soapy!' Saunders swung round. 'Catch!' A silver dollar flicked through the smoky atmosphere, beams of sunlight glinting off the shiny metallic surface.

With a deft hand common to all such lowlife denizens, he snatched the coin out of the air and bit down on it before slipping it into a pocket.

'Gee, thanks a bunch, Marshal,' fawned the soused swamper. It was rare for him to receive any tips at all, let alone a silver dollar. 'You sure are a gent and no mistake.'

Nevertheless, he rapidly disappeared into a back room just in case the marshal realized what he had just done.

'You oughtn't to have given him so much, marshal,' admonished Clancy drawing a tankard of beer for the lawman. 'Darned swamper'll be pesterin' all the customers now.'

Jonas shrugged off the barman's concern as he pushed another coin across the bar top.

The barman shook his head.

'On the house,' he said. 'We need some law around here now that the town's goin' places.'

'Tell me about this new mine,' enquired Jonas taking a welcome swig from the foaming pot. 'How can I find it?'

For the next half-hour, the bartender expanded Jonas's knowledge regarding the whole enterprise and its management. Two jugs of beer later, followed by a snort of bourbon, he bade his farewell thanking the bartender for his time.

'You're welcome, Marshal,' opined Clancy, resuming the ever present task of glass polishing. 'Anytime you've a mind, don't you hesitate to bend the ear of Shad Clancy.'

'I'll do that,' replied Jonas, leaving the saloon and returning to his office.

Earlier that morning his first delivery of mail had arrived by the weekly stagecoach from Durango. It contained a file of Wanted posters. Shuffling through the batch he came across the most interesting of the lot.

An artist's impression of Curly Ben Clovis stared back at him, and it bore a remarkably good likeness. A reward of $2,000 had been placed on the outlaw's head – dead or alive! A detailed outline of the Manzanola hold-up was followed by a sketchy profile of the perpetrators.

Jonas tensed when he came to his own description which included mention of his long blond hair. He would have to get it cut short. Nor was he too pleased that his bounty amounted to a meagre $300. A steely gleam crept into the hooded eyes. It lent credence to the curled lip essaying the notion that such a position would change significantly once the gang's current plans had been realized.

Yessirree! Jim Kane would make certain he was raised up a notch or two in the pecking order with a serious bounty to match.

Skimming through the rest of the pack, he nodded in recognition of a couple of names, but there were no other dodgers to cause any concern. Removing the ones purporting to the Clovis gang, he applied a lighted match to the edges and dropped them into the waste bin.

Over the course of the following week, Jim Kane (alias Jonas Kelly) settled himself into the unaccustomed routine of life on the side of law and order. After years of living with one eye open, always having to keep one step ahead of a pursuing posse, it took some getting used to.

There was little, however, to tax his grey matter.

On Tuesday, a fight between two drunken miners over a saloon girl ended up with them both cooling their heels overnight in the new cellblock. Jonas fined them each ten bucks, half of which he was able to retain.

Wednesday found him reprimanding a young boy who had been caught stealing apples from the general store. The kid's parents willingly coughed up the five-dollar fine which their wayward son would be paying off for the next few months by cleaning the store every night.

Thursday was the most interesting. The monthly delivery of silver from the Trujillo Mine needed an escort in addition to the driver and guard riding shotgun. This was one of the marshal's prescribed duties for which he astutely negotiated an additional fee claiming it was work undertaken outside his jurisdiction.

The route between the mine and Hashknife passed through constantly changing terrain ranging from open sagebrush plains to the shadowy cutting of Apache Pass. A blunt-edged north to south ridge of fractured sandstone had been cleaved asunder to form the only gap through which the silver could be transported.

It was an eerie place devoid of any sound. Even cawing buzzards and crows gave it a wide berth. Inside the rift, a chaotic splay of boulders littered the trail. At its narrowest point, there was barely sufficient width for a wagon to pass. At the far side of the pass, the trail divided. A weathered sign pointed the way west to Durango where the refiner was located.

The devious mind of Jim Kane, outlaw, instantly perceived that it was an ideal spot for an ambush. One more piece of useful information to store away.

The three-hour journey from the mine to Hashknife was accomplished without incident. On arrival the boxes of silver ore were quickly transferred to the bank vault.

Jonas made a point of chaperoning the operation from start to finish in order to figure out how best to purloin the valuable lucre. His questioning of the manager, Cranford Jagger, over a glass of French brandy passed without incident. As town marshal he could ensure that all angles would be covered in full without arousing any suspicion.

It soon became clear that breaking into the bank would prove a difficult and dangerous undertaking, especially with a twenty-four-hour guard in attendance. No such surmising was needed to conclude that the ideal spot for a hold-up was while the ore was in transit, and Apache Pass was where it would take place.

Having settled that vital piece of reasoning in his mind, all he could do now was await the gang's arrival, while trusting that the new lawdog did not turn up in the meantime. That would really set the cat among the pigeons.

To protect himself against such an unwelcome development, Jonas established a routine of taking an early morning ride. Ostensibly to scan out the lie of the land, once clear of Hashknife he turned east into the rising sun, that being the direction from which the genuine lawman would come.

After half an hour, he reached the lower slopes of Pueblo Bonito. From the front it was unassailable, the sheer cliff face rising over 500 feet and surrounded by a welter of dislodged rock debris. Circling behind however, Jonas had noticed a thin trail zig-zagging upward across the shattered ramparts. It offered a deceptively easy access to the concealed heights above where he found the remnants of a long abandoned

40

indian settlement after which the rocky butte was named.

Since being deserted ten years before, the village had fallen into disrepair. Wooden ladders still connected the various levels of mud brick apartments preserved in the dry atmosphere. But the empty rooms lent an air of decayed sadness to the place.

For hundreds of years, the strategic site had offered an effective defence for the Pueblo indians against other marauding tribes. But when faced with the lethal firepower of modern artillery, there was no protection.

While exploring the clutter of adobe dwellings, Jonas found numerous examples of brightly coloured pottery for which the indians were renowned. All very interesting, but to Jonas Kelly it afforded a perfect hideaway from which to observe the flat plains stretching away towards the eastern horizon.

So far the view had not revealed any undesirable visitors.

Another intriguing possibility had also presented itself at the foot of the butte. The old Indian trail afforded the perfect getaway once the silver had been lifted. Much overgrown and virtually undetectable, Jonas had followed it for an hour to ensure it headed in the right direction.

FIVE

JAILHOUSE ROCK

The new marshal's first Saturday night arrived.

Jonas knew from past experience that compared to the rest of the week, Saturday was always the liveliest. As it was in most other towns on the fringes of the western frontier, Hashknife would doubtless be no exception.

He made his rounds during the early part of the evening, checking that all premises were securely locked.

'Evening, Marshal,' Seth Torbin, the undertaker, was just locking up. 'A pleasant evening, is it not?'

'Sure is, Seth,' replied Jonas, his face split in a broad grin. He was enjoying this game. For that's what it was – a game of hide and seek, spot the outlaw, charades. But it was one that he knew would surely come to an end, and that day was not far distant. He shrugged the unsettling thought aside. For the present he was relishing the unaccustomed prestige that was part and parcel of the job.

At that moment, a group of riders galloped down the main street dragging their lathered mounts to a whinnying halt in a cloud of dust outside the saloon. Jonas recognized them as cowboys off the Lazy T spread judging by the brands on their mounts. He had heard tell they were a rough and ready outfit.

Yipping and heehawing, one of them spotted the lawman. Rocky Mason was ramrod and had earned his name on account of a pitted visage that closely resembled a coarsely weathered chunk of granite. A large, barrel-chested bruiser with a thick, dark moustache, he was clearly the mouthpiece of the group.

'Look who it is, boys,' he hollered loudly. 'The new marshal showin' off his shiny badge.'

The other five men all turned, hostile eyes following the direction of the pointing arm. The raucous hallooing died away. Grinning faces assumed the saturnine glower of children whose toys have been removed. Cowboys on a Saturday razzle and lawmen do not mix well.

'Don't look like much to me,' commented a sneering weasel by the name of Shorty Dobbs.

'Bin doin' a bit of polishin', Marshal?' pressed Mason, angling for a reaction to his jibes. 'That hunk of tin is sure glarin' on the eye.'

Sneering hoots of laughter followed Mason's caustic prod.

Jonas had been caught wrong-footed. This was new territory to him.

'Best keep out of the Silver Wheel tonight, Marshal,' continued Mason, hooking his thumbs provocatively into a tooled leather gunbelt. The other cowpokes ranged up behind him. Strength in numbers. 'Us Lazy T boys aim to enjoy ourselves without some tinstar tryin' to spoil our fun.'

'That is unless he's gonna buy all the drinks,' chuckled Dobbs, slapping his thigh in glee.

'Yahoo to that!' yipped Stringbean Calloway. The lanky critter suddenly drew his pistol and fired it into the air.

The sudden blast precipitated Seth Torbin into motion. He hurried off down the street in the opposite direction, anxious to be safely ensconsed inside his own home.

'Be seeing you, Marshal,' his quaking voice mumbled. 'Watch out for that Rocky Mason. He's big trouble.'

Jonas had already figured that out for himself. He knew the type. Indeed, many's the occasion when he had indulged in the same kind of star-baiting with the Clovis Gang.

Now he was on the receiving end.

How would he cope? Jonas knew it was a question that was bound to be answered sometime before daybreak. Maybe the job was not so enticing after all. Nevertheless, he stood his ground.

'Just so long as you boys keep yer noses clean,' he said in a flat even tone, 'you won't be seein' me.'

'Forget about him,' whined a stocky jasper removing his hat and slapping the dust from his leather

44

chaps. 'This dust has given me a raging thirst.'

The others muttered in agreement as the group shot a final glare in the marshal's direction before disdainfully stamping into the saloon.

Jonas let his breath out slowly. His first confrontation had passed off without incident. For that he was obliged. All the same, he decided to abandon his stroll around the town and made a beeline for his office.

It wasn't only thirsty cowboys who were feeling the need of a drink.

It was round eleven o'clock and the marshal was congratulating himself on the fact that the night had so far progressed without a hitch. Noise emanating from the Silver Wheel had grown steadily in volume, but that was to be expected on a Saturday night.

Jonas reached for a bottle of bourbon, then hesitated before putting it away in the filing cabinet. There was still a heap of raucous celebrating left in the night, and he figured it prudent to remain alert should any trouble flare up.

Instead, he settled back in his chair with a mug of coffee and a plate of pastries kindly brought round by Molly Haskins from the Glad Tidings Diner. His mouth watered in anticipation.

But even before he had time to take the first bite the office door slammed back on its hinges and the saloon swamper hustled in. Unused to the exertion of having run across the whole width of Main Street, Soapy Saunders was breathing heavily. Watery eyes bulged wide as he clutched at his hammering ticker.

Jonas stared open-mouthed, agog.

'You gotta come quick, Marshal,' the swamper panted, strugging to catch his breath. 'Things is gettin' ugly over there.' He vaguely waved an arm in the general direction of the Silver Wheel.

'What's happened?' exclaimed Jonas grabbing his hat and buckling on his gunhelt. The tasty treat was reluctantly placed to one side.

'That skunk Mason threw a bottle and smashed the mirror behind the bar. He claimed the whiskey that Clancy sold him had been watered down.' Soapy shook his head. 'Poor old Shad had that mirror brought all the way from Denver. Must have cost a fortune. And it were his pride and joy. Now its just a heap of broken glass.'

'Never mind that,' urged Jonas, checking the chambers of his revolver. He then selected a shotgun from the rack and slotted two cartridges into the twin barrels. 'Has anybody been hurt?'

Soapy's scrawny head bobbed like a fishing float.

'Mason slugged Clancy when he objected. The guy's bleedin' bad from a head wound.'

That was when a flurry of shots rang out from the saloon.

'What in tarnation is that?' snapped the marshal rushing to the door.

'The bastard reckoned he was gonna shoot the candles off the crystal chandelier. He musta started already.'

Soapy followed the marshal across the street, albeit at a slower rather tentative pace. After all, he was only

46

a swamper, and had no desire to become a target in Rocky Mason's shooting gallery.

Jonas paused outside the saloon. He needed time to figure out how best to deal with this. But time was not on his side as Saunders urgently reminded him.

'That varmint's gonna kill somebody if'n he ain't stopped,' wailed the swamper, cowering behind the broad back of the marshal.

'OK! OK!' snapped Jonas. 'This needs careful handlin'.'

He didn't need the town drunk giving him orders. Cautiously peering over the batwing doors, he could see Rocky Mason taking aim at the chandelier. His sidekicks were egging him on.

All eyes were fixed on the light.

Jonas pushed through the door, the shotgun in one hand and his revolver in the other.

Immediately he could see that Rocky Mason was no gunslick. The cap and ball Navy Colt clutched in his right hand was old, the barrel pitted with rust. Clearly it had not been cleaned in a coon's age. Mason was just a loud-mouthed braggart showing off to his buddies.

'Drop the gun, Mason,' growled Jonas, injecting the order with a biting touch of venom. 'Didn't I tell yuh to keep the peace?'

The cowboy slewed round, his face blotchy and puffed with drink. He might not have been a gunfighter, but too much hard liquor made him a dangerous opponent.

A scoffing leer cloaked the soused visage.

'Think you got the guts to take it off me, Marshal?' he drawled, waving the ancient firearm with menacing intent. The ramrod beckoned the lawman forward, scornfully inviting him to remove the gun if he had the nerve.

The pair faced one another, alone.

Mason's cronies had stepped back out of the line of fire. The imminent threat of gunplay had quickly sobered them.

'Just be sensible,' urged Jonas quietly, 'and we can settle this without anyone getting hurt.'

Mason let out a raucous guffaw. 'Yer a yeller skunk, mister.' He leaned forward scowling. 'And I reckon yuh oughta crawl back into yer pit and let us real men carry on enjoyin' ourselves.'

Jonas knew that he had to do something quickly, not only to neutralize the situation but to maintain his own reputation. The longer this carried on the more chance Mason's buddies had of recovering their nerve and joining in. That scenario could only end in blood-shed and tears.

His gaze shifted to a position behind the swagger-ing cowpoke.

'You take him from behind, Bill,' he muttered.

Normally such a blatant attempt at diversionary tactics would have been received with disbelief and mocking derision. No sober adversary would have been taken in. But Mason was drunk and the ruse worked perfectly.

His yawing mouth hung open as he swung round. This gave Jonas the opportunity to step in quickly and slug the jigger over the head with the butt of his revolver.

Mason emitted a startled grunt as he staggered under the heavy blow. His gun erupted, the bullet ploughing into a lantern hanging from the low ceiling. It shattered into a myriad pieces.

But the ramrod was not finished. The numbing effect of the liquor had cushioned the stunning blow. A rabid growl erupted from the cowboy's bleeding head as he desperately tried to recock the pistol. A second brisk thwack of wood on bone did the trick.

Mason threw up his arms, the old gun clattering to the floor. He swayed wildly, then slumped to his knees before keeling over.

But all was still not yet over.

Shorty Dobbs was incensed.

'Dirty rotten skunk,' he growled. 'Yer tricked him.'

Mason was his buddy. They had ridden together for the last three years. With a growl of anger, Dobbs drew his own pistol and fired. Flame and hot lead burst from the long barrel of the .36 Whitney. Had he paused to take proper aim, Jonas Kelly would have been consigned to oblivion, a candidate for the ministrations of Seth Torbin.

But Dobbs was no less inebriated than his thick-skulled confederate. That said, his aim was not far off the mark. His shot plucked the hat from the lawman's head. Unthinking, Jonas swung the heavy shotgun round in a tight arc and let fly with both barrels.

Dobbs stood no chance. He was lifted clean off his feet and slammed back against the wall. An ugly red smear was left behind as the peppered cowpoke's body slid to the floor.

'Anyone else got a beef with my way of keeping the peace?' he shouted.

The new marshal was well and truely riled up. His eyes glowed with a fiery resonance. The brittle retort echoed round the now silent room. Slowly, the thick pall of gunsmoke dispersed to reveal the other customers emerging from beneath tables and any other place of concealment they could find.

Nobody spoke as the cocked revolver panned the room.

'Somebody get this turkey down to the undertaker's,' rapped the marshal stiffly. Then he curtly ordered Stringbean Calloway and another of the Lazy T boys to pick Mason up off the floor and lug him over to the jail.

Before the remaining cowpokes left, he said, 'Party's over, boys. You can go on home now. Tell the boss that he can collect this lump of turd tomorrow after he's sobered up. Now skedaddle pronto.' His voice rose an octave as he finished. 'And don't be givin' me no grief next week. Savvy?'

'S-sure thing, Marshal,' stuttered the nervous pair backing out of the door. 'You won't get no trouble from us agin'. No sir!'

'And you can also tell the boss that he better bring a heap of dough with him.' Calloway looked askance. 'For the fine and the damages.'

Vigorous nods of assent saw the cowboys hurrying to their tethered mounts.

Once they had departed, Jonas hurried across to the jailhouse to see that his new guest was well settled. Then he took out the bottle of whiskey and sank gratefully into his cushioned chair. Hoisting his spurred boots on to the scarred desktop, he splashed a generous measure into a glass.

Well heck, didn't he deserve it? A wry smile broke across the taciturn façade. He sipped the golden spirit appreciatively, its warm glow helping to relax tight muscles. Cocking an ear towards the street outside, he listened.

Silence.

Now that's what I call a good night's work, he mused.

SIX

BAD NEWS TRAVELS FAST

Nothing untoward ever happened on a Sunday.

Respectable folks attended church while the saloon denizens rubbed sore heads and spent the day recovering from the previous night's excesses.

That included Rocky Mason who was snoring loudly in the cellblock. Jonas curled his lip. The hardcase could stay there until somebody from the Lazy T ranch came by to bail him out. A more sombre thought was that the body of Shorty Dobbs would need to be disposed of at some point. That might take a little more explaining.

Jonas was likewise recovering from having scraped through his first major incident as town marshal. He stepped out of the office stretching his long limbs. One of Molly Haskins's breakfasts was needed along with a pot of strong coffee.

A stiff breeze propelled a couple of recalcitrant tumbleweeds down the street. They were followed by a buggy trotting at a more sedate pace. A shiver ran down the marshal's spine on recognizing the driver. The arrival of Rachel Summers riding down the main street was a tonic he desperately needed. His thumping heart leapt at the sight of the lithe figure pulling up in front of the general store.

No time was wasted as he hurried across the street.

Titian hair tied back in a green bow perfectly squared with the scintillating emerald of her dazzling eyes. The figure-hugging shirt, open at the neck, revealed more than a hint of tanned cleavage. Jonas struggled to keep his bulging peepers from straying as he helped her down.

'Much obliged, Marshal,' smiled the girl, oblivious to the mesmerizing effect she had precipitated.

'I didn't expect to see you in Hashknife again so soon, Miss Summers,' croaked Jonas, coughing to hide his nervousness. He was unused to mixing with ladies of her pedigree. More at home in red-light districts, the outlaw normally paid for the dubious pleasure of female company. 'You are looking extremely fetching today.'

Rachel's cheeks coloured slightly at the compliment. Nevertheless, she welcomed it.

Her father had specifically commented upon the extra care she had taken with her appearance that morning. Make-up and lip rouge were usually reserved for a Saturday dance. She had managed to allay his curiosity by claiming a lunch date with her friend Sandy Flockhart, the mayor's daughter. In truth, she had hoped to be able to resume her conversation with the new law officer at the earliest opportunity.

'Well, thank you, sir,' she said, raising her long silky eyebrows. There was a catch in her throat. The blood pounded in her veins. He was just as handsome as she had thought initially. A little rough around the edges, but that only added to his fascination. 'I needed to make another visit to town to buy in extra supplies for the spring round-up.'

Jason removed his hat, nervously twirling it between in his fingers.

'Erm,' he stammered feeling decidedly awkward. 'After you've completed your business' – he paused unsure of himself, then ploughed on, the words tumbling out in a flood – 'perhaps you might be agreeable to having a late breakfast with me?'

Shuffling his feet he anxiously waited for the girl's reaction. Each second seemed like an hour.

'That would be my pleasure, Marshal.' Her dulcet tones, chirpy and lilting like a song thrush, were music to Jonas's ears. His heart sang in unison. 'Shall we meet at the diner in say . . . one hour?'

Jonas could only manage a vague nod. The girl's parting smile turned his legs to jelly.

As Rachel Summers walked away, Jonas Kelly noticed a few grinning faces nudging one another suggestively. He squared his broad shoulders, the lantern jaw set in a determined glower. Then, drawing himself up to his full height of six feet two, he stamped back across the street to his office.

That was when it struck him. What in tarnation was he playing at? A no-account desperado playing at marshal and attempting to woo the prettiest girl in town. He must be crazy, a durned fool. There could never be any future for such a liaison. Any day now, the whole of the dubious deception could come tumbling down around his ears.

His only hope was to prevent the new lawman from reaching Hashknife. From his daily lookout perch atop Pueblo Bonita, he would have ample opportunity to arrange a terminal reception for the unwelcome starpacker.

Such morbid reflections were cut short by the arrival of Gripper Taggart, the owner of the Lazy T. He was a bluff Scotsman with a broad accent to match his florid appearance. Accompanying the rancher were a couple of hired hands. Jonas couldn't help noticing that they were each toting a pair of six-shooters in low-slung crossed gunbelts.

'I think you have my foreman locked up in one of your cells,' Taggart rapped, gruffly disposing of the usual formalities. 'If Mason has caused any damage to the saloon, it'll be docked from his wages.'

'He'll have a sore head this morning,' replied the lawman. 'And not only from the amount of liquor he sank.'

'I heard that you felt the need to slug him,' challenged the rancher brusquely.

'It was his choice.'

'I heard that as well.'

Jonas relaxed. It appeared that this blunt rancher was well aware of his foreman's shortcomings.

'It'll cost you fifty bucks to spring him,' said the marshal holding the other man with a steadfast regard. 'Payable in advance.'

Taggart didn't flinch. He stuck a hand inside his jacket and removed a thick billfold. Peeling off the greenbacks, he passed them over.

'Follow me,' said Jason accepting the fine. 'You need to sign him out.'

Five minutes later, the lamentable figure of Rocky Mason emerged from the jailhouse. Taggart's granite-faced expression, bleak and hectoring, intimated that the ramrod was in for a severe tongue-lashing.

Jonas allowed himself a brief smirk as he pocketed his share of the proceeds. It would more than pay for the meal he had booked at the Glad Tidings Diner.

Breakfast passed in a dream for Jonas. Afterwards, he could barely recall anything. He must have said all the right things, managing somehow to keep his distress under wraps. Rachel had laughed and chattered away completely unaware of the pain that was perniciously eating away at his insides.

They parted agreeing to do the same again in the near future. The notion passed through his mind as to whether that eventuality would ever come to pass. It was a morose reflection he could not dispel.

He helped Rachel on to the buggy and was about to wave her off when a rider galloped down the middle of the street at full tilt. His mount slithered to an ungainly halt beside the buggy. Steam rose in clouds from the animal's lathered flanks. It had clearly been ridden hard.

Rachel gasped in surprise.

'Windy!' exclaimed the girl. 'Why are you in such an all-fired hurry?'

'It's yer pa, Miss Rachel,' gabbled the lean, rangy guy as he tried to regain his breath. 'He's bin shot, and rustlers have taken that new batch of cayuses we'd broken in.'

Windy Rivers was a part-time hand on the Summers Horse Ranch. He occupied an old line cabin up on the Villegreen Plateau some five miles from the ranch where he kept chickens and a few pigs. He also helped with the bronc busting when the need arose. The rest of his time was devoted to tending a smallholding that Buck Summers had given him.

Rachel had never quite figured out the substance of their relationship. All she knew was that Windy Rivers and her father had been in the same regiment during the war, and Rivers had saved her father's life.

'Pa's been shot?' gasped Rachel, her eyes widening in disbelief. 'I only left the ranch at sun-up and he was fine then.'

'Them devils musta bin a-waitin' to pounce,' Rivers said. Then seeing the distress emblazoned on the girl's face he hurried on attempting to assuage the frightful news. 'He ain't dead though. The skunks shot him twice, but yer pa's a tough old buzzard. I fixed him up best as I could before hightailin' it down here. He'll need the doc to sort him out proper. But I figured the marshal needed to be told lickety-split.'

Jonas had been taking all this in and quickly took the reins.

'You did right, fella,' he agreed, adopting a practised stance as if this sort of occurrence was nothing out of the ordinary. If only they knew. 'I take it that you weren't there when this happened,' he said, peering closely at the grizzled bronc buster.

'I only arrived mid mornin' to tackle a couple of feisty stallions that had been givin' us trouble.' He threw his arms wide. 'But there weren't no mustangs in the corral. Not a one.'

'Any idea which direction they took?' Jonas shot back, anxious to show his concern for the situation. His brain was ticking over fast. If he could sort this business out, Rachel would surely be beholden to him.

Once again he had forgotten about the silver heist, the girl's pleading look washing all else from his thoughts.

The bronc buster scratched at the few remaining hairs on his bald pate. Screwing up his wrinkled face he sighed, 'Didn't think to look. But they're bound to have left a clear trail seein' as how they're a-drivin' twenty mustangs.'

'Then we better get out there right away afore the trail goes cold. First off though, I need to organize a posse.'

'Count me in,' announced Rivers with fervid zeal.

Jonas nodded approvingly.

'I must get back to the ranch straight away,' interrupted a distraught Rachel climbing briskly on to the buggy. 'See how bad Pa's been hit.'

All starry-eyed thoughts of a romantic entangle-ment with the marshal were forgotten as she hallooed the horse into motion. Jonas wished her well, but his words were whipped away by the haunting refrain of the wind.

He then hurried inside the office to secure extra ammunition for the Henry.

Waiting for him was a special delivery from the state capital in Denver. It must have arrived while he was at the Glad Tidings. Addressed to the legal representa-tive, the contents were an unexpected if pleasant surprise. Along with three new Colt .45s, was a pair of Winchester rifles with extended octagonal barrels.

Lovingly, Jonas caressed the shiny rosewood stock of the new repeater. His eyes gleamed. For a jasper who'd spent all his adult life dodging the law, it was a mind-boggling experience to be presented with the latest and best firearms. Slowly, he opened one of the cartridge boxes and thumbed the rounds into the side housing. A quick up-and-down of the lever and the weapon was primed and ready.

It felt good in his hands, perfectly balanced. Not like the old Henry which was only fit for scrap now, not to mention his Army Remington.

A louring frown elbowed aside the euphoric mood of minutes before. He quickly surmised that the new law officer must have ordered the weapons. It was a cogent reminder of the transient nature of his posi-tion in this town. Checking out the guns, he deter-mined that one of each would be leaving with him when the time came for a swift departure from Hashknife.

He sighed. This job really did have its advantages. He would be sorry to depart. He would be even sorrier to leave the alluring presence of the lovely Rachel Summers. But there was no sense in mooning over what might have been.

As for the here and now, he had some rustlers to catch.

The next stop was the office of the town council where he quickly and concisely explained the situation to the town's leading citizen.

In small towns dotted across the western frontier, it was common practice for permanent residents to be asked to join a posse if such was required of them. The payment of an attendance fee meant that such groups were often easily recruited.

Within a half-hour, six candidates had assembled outside the council offices where the mayor solemnly read out the legal requirement for a deputization. In conclusion, each man raised his right hand and declared his dedication to the task with the steadfast affirmation, 'I do!'

Soapy Saunders' voice was the loudest. It had been a surprise to the saloon swamper when the marshal had agreed to his becoming a member of the posse, much to the dismay of Elmer Flockhart who had vigorously objected. Saunders had claimed to have been a sharpshooter during the war. To test out the claim, the marshal had set up a line of tin cans behind the jailhouse. Soapy had brought along his old .44 Spencer rifle.

Potting four out of the five with barely a pause between each shot decided the issue. Soapy was in.

The men were then given glossy new badges which they each brazenly pinned to their vests in prominent positions for all the other citizens to see.

Once the little ceremony had been conducted, Jonas Kelly led the posse of six deputies out of town in the direction of the Summers Ranch.

SEVEN

RUSTLERS

Two hours later, the small group of riders entered the San Cristobal Valley. Cresting a low rise, they dropped down a shallow grade where the grazing pastures of the Summers Ranch opened up before them. Fenced off corrals abutted the main house and barn.

But all were empty. It was obvious that the old bronc buster had not exaggerated the seriousness of the situation.

In front of the house was Rachel's buggy. On hearing the hoofbeats of the posse, she came outside accompanied by her father.

Buck Summers was a tall, solidly built man with iron-grey hair and a well-trimmed goatee beard. His close-fitting embroidered jacket and tight trousers were in the tradition of a Mexican grandee. There was no denying that the rancher was an imposing figure. The powder-blue eyes remained clear and focused, a cogent indication that his traumatic experience at the hands of the raiders had in no way dented his will and determination, although it was obvious from the stooped shoulders and ashen features that the injuries had taken their toll on the ageing rancher.

After dismounting, Jonas led the sorrel over to a water trough. The other members of the posse did likewise. Returning to the open veranda fronting the ranch house, he wasted no time in idle chatter.

'You had better tell me what happened, Mr Summers,' he said bluntly.

Assisted by his daughter, Summers sank gratefully into a chair. Before answering, he accepted a glass of home-made fruit juice and gestured for the posse to help themselves to the glasses laid out on a table.

'Help yourselves, gentlemen.' The measured tone was quiet and dignified. Here was a man used to the authority of military command. 'Rachel has also prepared some vittles while you hunt down these varmints.' His grey eyes clouded over. 'That's wild country out there and it might take some time.'

'Is there much you can tell us?' pressed Jonas.

The old rancher paused to gather his thoughts.

'They must have been waiting for Rachel to leave the valley before making their move,' he rasped, struggling to contain a burning anger. 'Segundo Mesa would have blocked off all sounds of their attack. It was the snickering of the mustangs that alerted me. Fully broke horses don't cause that sort of ruckus. When I came out on to the veranda, these men were herding them out of the corral. As mean a bunch of varmints as I ever did see.'

'How many were there?' asked Jonas.

Summers squinted in thought. 'I counted three at the back and another two acting as point riders. Soon as I saw what they were doing, I shouted at them to stop.' He shook his head. 'Not like me at all. Shoulda gone back inside and got me a buffalo gun, then picked them off.' His head dropped on to his heaving chest. 'Guess I panicked. They took me by surprise.'

'It wasn't your fault, Dad.' Rachel put her arms around the sagging shoulders trying to offer some comfort to the distraught man.

' 'Course not, Buck,' interjected Windy Rivers. 'Any one of us woulda done the same.' Nods of accord backed up the old buster's platitude. 'They didn't give you a chance.'

Summers carried on. No amount of verbal featherbedding could console him.

'Didn't even have a derringer on me,' he grunted. 'I just stood there hollering at them like a durned fool. When I moved down from the veranda and started across the yard the guy in charge rode forward barging me down.'

'What was he like?' posed Jonas.

'A cold-hearted mountain of a man with a red beard. He just laughed in my face. Then he pulled out his pistol and shot me, cool as you please. Didn't say a word.' The rancher paused for breath. The narration had sapped what little energy he had left. His eyes misted over.

'That's enough,' snapped Rachel, her sharp retort

aimed at Jonas. 'He needs to rest before I take him into Hashknife to see the doctor.'

'Sure, sure,' agreed the marshal anxious not to rile this feisty female beauty. 'Don't suppose you saw which way they went, did you?'

The rancher didn't reply. A pained grimace arced across the distingushed features, his right hand clutching at the shoulder wound. Instead, he turned in his chair and pointed to the north.

'Much obliged, sir,' Jonas thanked him whilst offering Rachel a supportive look. 'We'll get them. You can be sure of that. Won't we, boys?'

'Sure will, Mr Summers,' echoed back from the posse as they set their glasses down and prepared to leave.

After mounting up, Jonas led the posse out of the yard heading north.

Windy Rivers had been right. The trail was easy to follow. A mite too easy if truth be told, mused Jonas. These rustlers didn't appear in the slightest bit concerned that a posse would be on their tail.

All through the rest of the morning and well into the afternoon, the group of riders kept up a steady pace along a trail that was over ten yards wide in places. A blind man could follow it. Dipping and weaving between clumps of thornhush and beavertail cactus, it led them ever further northwards.

'We oughta be gettin' a sight of 'em soon.' It was late afternoon. The sun was drifting down towards the western horizon when Soapy Saunders voiced the thoughts of all the others, including the marshal.

'There ain't even a flicker of their dust.' The throaty baritone of Hank Rogers cast a gloomy pall over the posse.

Jonas frowned. Something was wrong here. But he couldn't figure out what it was. That irritating burr on his neck was telling him to be wary. And it had never let him down before. He gave it a brisk scratch.

'Keep your eyes peeled, boys,' he ordered, earnestly scanning the terrain for any sign of skulduggery. 'These jaspers might have us in their sights at this very minute.'

This notion brought a ripple of dismay from the plodding line of riders. The enthusiasm evident at the start of the pursuit was fast dissolving.

It was another hour when the trail abruptly disappeared. The posse had just rounded a craggy knoll. One minute they were following a broad swathe of hoofprints, the next . . . zero.

The sandy expanse was smooth as a fishing pond. Consternation gripped the posse. They peered around uncertainly, guns drawn.

Well versed in the devious minds of those who followed the owlhoot trail, Jonas immediately surmised that they had been tricked. The rustlers had deliberately led them on a wild goose chase. The jaspers must have deviated from the trail with the main herd of mustangs while a couple of their number had carried on heading north to lay a false scent for the unwitting pursuers to follow blindly.

And it had succeeded. Jonas cursed aloud.

'When they branched off earlier, the scheming

66

varmints must have brushed out their sign,' suggested Windy Rivers, voicing what Jonas had been thinking. 'And they could have only gone west,' he added dragging his horse about in readiness to retrace their steps.

'How d'yuh figure that?' asked a young guy who helped out at the livery stable. Kansas Pete had discovered the hard way that he couldn't handle the confined space of working underground in the silver mine – the sawbones had called it claustrophobia. Just the thought of those dark, cramped levels brought him out in a cold sweat.

Working with horses in the livery stable was a dream come true which is why Pete had volunteered for the posse.

'If they'd gone east, we would have seen their dust,' replied the bronc buster to Pete's query. 'Them sagebrush plains is too flat to hide a jack-rabbit.'

The marshal nodded his agreement. 'And I reckon it can't have been too far back else we'd have spotted them,' he concluded, stepping down off the sweating sorrel. 'Anyway, it's too late for us to backtrack tonight. Them tricky gophers have worked this out good. We'll have to camp here tonight and set off back at first light.'

Rivers set about building a fire. But it would be a cold supper: Jonas had miscalculated, not anticipating a night away from Hashknife. It was lucky that Rachel Summers had seen fit to provide them with some tasty vittles.

The sun was well over the eastern rim of the distant

Sangre de Cristo range as the dispirited posse set off back along the trail. An air of melancholy hung in the cool air of early morn.

Jonas knew that it was up to him to rectify his mistake of the previous day. He couldn't help conjecturing that a more experienced law officer would have anticipated such a move by the rustlers.

The ride back was at a much slower pace as the men keenly scanned the ground for any sign that might indicate where the rustlers had pulled their deception.

It was Windy Rivers who drew them to a halt beside a cluster of desiccated greasewood trees. He knew this part of the territory well. Indicating for the others to stay on the trail, he circled around behind the clump of trees. It was ten minutes later that a whoop of triumph pierced the air.

The old soldier returned soon after, a beaming grin splitting the seamed contours of his weather-beaten features.

'What did yuh find?' enquired the tense marshal.

Rivers answered with a pointing arm.

'See that rock mesa behind the trees?' He didn't wait for a reply. 'Well that's Blind Man's Bluff. It marks the entrance to a hidden canyon called Redrock Alley.' His enthusiastic dialogue had gripped the attention of the faded posse. 'From here it don't look like there's a way through, but it's an optical illusion, a trick of nature. And one that this crafty bunch of rustlers have used to their advantage. Once I was out of sight round the trees, the horse trail restarted, clear as a mountain stream.'

'OK, listen up, boys!' Jonas was determined to reassert his authority. 'Check your weapons. We need to be extra vigilant from here on.' His next query was aimed at the bronc buster. 'How long is this ravine?' he asked.

'No more than three miles,' replied Rivers. 'Once you're through the tapered neck, it opens up into a broad amphitheatre called the Saguache Basin. I reckon that's where these guys will have the mustangs penned up. My figurin' is they'll wait until a decent-sized herd's bin gathered, then drive 'em south over the border into New Mexico.'

'Where will they sell broke nags?' asked Soapy Saunders thumbing back the hammer of his rifle to ascertain there was a shell up the spout.

'Ain't you got no sense in that soused brain?' scoffed the blacksmith. The swamper was not well regarded by the more affluent citizens of Hashknife. 'The soldier boys at Fort Union are cryin' out for good horseflesh.'

'And there's allus Fort Sumner,' added the livery hand. 'No shortage of willing buyers there.'

'Let's go then,' ordered Jonas nudging his mount forward. 'You ride alongside me, Windy, seeing as how you know the place.'

Tentatively, the posse edged forward, all eagle-eyed, muscles strung tight with gagged tension. Strain was clearly etched across the seven brooding faces. This was where possemen earned their fee.

Redrock Alley was well named. A chaotic splurge of

boulders littered the narrow passage forcing the riders into single file. Splashes of yellow-flowered prickly pear relieved the harsh glare of the brittle landscape.

Around noon the constricted draw widened perceptibly as they emerged into the broad flat bowl of the Saguache Basin.

EIGHT

SAGUACHE SHOWDOWN

Jonas signalled a halt.

Dismounting, he quickly scuttled up a nearby outcrop to survey the surrounding terrain. Eyes screwed tight against the harsh glare, he scanned the enclosed basin of the Saguache. It offered the perfect hideout for rustled stock.

And there they were. About a half-mile ahead, he could see the mustangs enclosed within a zig-zagged snake fence. To the right of the pen, some fifty wards away, smoke from a camp-fire rose into the still air. Moving about the camp, he counted five men. There was no cabin, indicating this was merely a temporary stopover.

Jonas nodded to himself. He had been part of a similar operation in the Texas Panhandle where it was cattle rather than horses that were on the hoof. He felt sure that the fire would contain running irons to alter brands. More likely in this case was that the gang would have their own brand seeing as the mustangs had only just been broken.

Returning to the waiting posse, he passed on what he had seen.

'How we gonna take 'em, Marshal?' posed Kansas Pete, who was eager for some action now they had caught up with their quarry.

'We're gonna leave the nags here and go in on foot,' he said with fervour, dragging the new Winchester from its boot and jacking a round into the breech. Confidence in his new job had been restored. His error regarding the lost trail was now history. The next order was to Windy Rivers. 'You take Saunders, Hank and the kid. Circle around to the left. And keep to the higher ground then you'll have the advantage of lookin' down on the camp. Savvy?'

'You betcha, Marshal,' Rivers shot back. He was keen to get moving. To the old soldier, it was just like old times when he and Buck Summers used to furtively penetrate enemy lines during the war.

'And don't shoot until I give the signal,' cautioned Jonas, as the three men took off across the rough terrain. 'The rest of us will go right. That way we trap them in a crossfire if they refuse to surrender.'

'You ain't gonna give them thievin' rats a chance, are yuh, Marshal?' queried the assay clerk scornfully. 'Save us a heap of trouble if'n we just wipe the lot of 'em out.'

Jonas speared the man with a look of icy disdain.

'You do as you're told, Gartside,' he hissed through clenched teeth. 'I'll decide how we play this, not you.' The acerbic rebuke was forthright and uncompromising. 'Besides, I want a prisoner so as to find out if they're operatin' alone or with a syndicate.' His dark gaze pinned the clerk down. 'You understand me, fella?'

'Of course, Marshal,' stuttered the chastened man, backing off. 'Just askin' is all.'

Without further delay, Jonas led his party between stands of blooming yucca interspersed with untidy clusters of rocks. Numerous clumps of bunched grama grass sprouted at intervals affording feed for the concealed stock.

'Keep your heads down,' he whispered, as they drew nearer to the camp. 'Don't want them jiggers eyeballing us and spoiling the surprise.'

When they were less than a hundred yards from the camp, Jason signalled to Rafe Gartside to scramble up on to a rocky ledge where he could act as cover when Jonas made his play. He intended to crawl the last fifty yards before calling on the gang to surrender. If they chose to ignore the offer, then Rafe Gartside might well get his wish.

The marshal waited until the assay clerk was halfway up a boulder-choked gully that led to a rocky overhang before gingerly moving off towards the nearby camp. The rustlers were all clearly in view. Any thoughts that the hideaway might have been rumbled had been relegated to the backburner. Their attention was completely absorbed in the onerous task of preparing the branding irons.

Jonas was almost in position when a sharp cry broke out to his rear. Twisting round he saw the ungainly figure of Rafe Gartside desperately clinging to a rocky protuberance. He had lost his footing and precipitated a minor avalanche of loose stones. The clattering noise reverberated around the enclosed basin effectively curtailing the surprise which Jonas had been counting on.

'What's that?'

The harsh demand from one of the gang saw the five rustlers peering anxiously towards the rocky over-hang where Gartside was splayed out like a lizard on a wall.

'We've bin rumbled!' exclaimed one of them.

'Grab yer guns, boys!' hollered a burly jasper with thick red hair and a beard to match. 'Take cover.'

Gartside didn't stand a chance. He was cut down by a volley of rifle fire, four neat holes appearing in his back. Arms flung wide he tumbled headlong off the rock face.

On the far side of the camp, Windy Rivers had quickly taken in the situation and ordered his own men to open fire. Two of the gang were cut down straight away as they ran for their horses. Like discarded rag dolls they toppled into the dust and lay still. A disturbed hare bolted across the open ground disappearing into a clump of sagebrush. Squawking buzzards lifted into the hot air, anxious to distance themselves from the gun battle.

The other three rustlers quickly sought out what limited cover was available. Caught in the open clearing between the two sets of attackers, they were forced to hunker down behind their saddles.

Jonas leapt from behind a stand of juniper trees and snapped off a couple of wild shots. He was rewarded with a flurry of rifle fire that quickly drove him back into cover. Slivers of flaking wood flew in all directions.

He hugged the base of the tree. For a full minute he remained still, unmoving, trying to determine how best to proceed now that the posse's surprise advantage had been frustrated.

Careful to avoid being spotted he peeped out and cast a bleak eye towards the huddled outlaws. One of the rustlers had decided that a cluster of rocks on the far side of the camp afforded more protection. Jonas emptied his revolver at the scurrying figure. Only with his final round did he have the satisfaction of hearing a pained yelp as the rustler hit the dust.

'I'm hit, Red,' croaked the injured man. 'He got me in the leg.'

Dragging the shattered limb behind him, the outlaw desperately clawed his way across the open ground. Inches from cover, another shot from the far side of the clearing slammed into his head. The man's skull exploded like a ripe melon, blood and gore spilling from the horrific wound.

The brutal sight was accompanied by a shout of excited chortling from Soapy Saunders.

'Yahoo! Got the bastard!' hollered the swamper

waving his arms around windmill fashion. 'This Spencer might be old but it still does the business.' Soapy's vociferous cheer was followed by a spot of personal back-slapping. 'And you sure ain't lost yer touch neither, have yuh, Soapy?'

But the swamper's euphoria had made him throw caution to the wind. His grinning mug couldn't resist gaping at the source of his elation from over the top of the houlder behind which he was secreted.

'Keep yer head down, yer darned fool!'

But Windy Rivers' warning came seconds too late.

Red Chandler mouthed an unintelligible curse and took careful aim. The rustler was no slouch himself when it came to gunplay. And one bullet was all he needed to silence Soapy Saunders' yammering expletives for good.

For the next half-hour, bullets were exchanged but no fresh advantage was accrued by either faction. The posse had the distinct advantage of better cover and more firepower. They also had access to water so it was only a matter of waiting until the desert heat took its toll.

With only two of them left, Red Chandler knew that his only hope lay in sticking it out until nightfall, then trying to sneak out under cover of darkness.

His partner had less backbone. For the last five minutes Butte Scanlon had been carping on about their hopeless situation. His spineless whinging was starting to get on Chandler's nerves.

Then it happened.

'I'm gettin' out of here,' announced a panic-stricken Scanlon. 'This place is too hot for me.'

Ducking low, he scampered across the open ground to his mount. The large bay mare was the only one that had been left saddled. Bullets from the posse plucked at his sleeve, but none found its mark.

Red Chandler's lip curled in a derisory sneer.

'Nobody ducks out on me,' he growled to himself, drawing a bead on Scanlon's weaving back with his rifle. He allowed the man to clamber into the saddle, then coolly pulled the trigger as the fleeing rustler passed by in a cloud of dust no more than ten feet away. An ugly smirk crinkled Chandler's hardened features as the fatal round slammed into Scanlon's back.

Spread-eagled behind his saddle with barely enough cover for a jaybird, the big man was rapidiy coming to the conclusion that his options were becoming slimmer by the minute. The rustler's throat was drier than a temperance bar. But at least he had a full canteen. It had been replenished only minutes before this danged posse cut loose.

His hand reached for the canteen. It felt too light. Then he saw it: a ragged hole from a stray bullet.

Empty.

Damn and blast. Lurid curses of every hue and description burst from Red Chandler's ranting mouth.

To hell with it, he thought. Now that he was the only gang member left alive, he decided to go out in a paroxysm of glory, all guns blazing. No way was he going to end his days swinging from a rope's end.

77

Quickly he loaded his remaining shells into the six-shooter. His rifle was empty with no spare ammo within reach. He threw it aside.

Over to his right, Jonas Kelly knew that the man called Red was the only rustler left unscathed. So he decided to give him the chance to surrender, just like he had intended before Gartside blew their cover.

Chandler was all set to make his move when a sharp voice echoed across the clearing.

'Hold yer fire, boys,' the marshal called out loud enough for Rivers and his remaining two men to hear. 'I got a proposition for this jasper.'

Chandler paused as the firing died away, then sank back on to his haunches.

'You hear me, fella?' Jonas called to the outlaw. 'I'll make you a deal if you surrender right now.'

'Why should I believe you?' countered Chandler. He was deeply suspicious that these guys were only after the bounty on his head. 'Dead or alive, the poster says. It'll be a whole lot simpler for you just to cut me down soon as I stand up.'

'You got the wrong end of the stick, mister,' replied Jonas. 'I'm a peace officer from Hashknife and these other guys are my posse. You give yourself up and I'll see to it you get a fair trial and the circuit judge knows you surrendered of your own accord. He's bound to go easy on you. And you'll be saving the town the expense of a hanging. So what d'you say? Is it a deal?' He paused before adding in a sombre almost apologetic tone, 'I guess you've already figured out what the alternative is.'

Jonas Kelly was indeed sympathetic to the rustler's plight. He had been in a similar position before. Only on that occasion, Curly Ben and the gang had shot their way out of trouble and escaped to fight another day. Red Chandler did not have that option.

The marshal waited for a minute, then repeated his offer. 'What's it gonna be, fella? Dead or Alive?'

'OK, Marshal,' he shouted, 'I'm comin' out. Tell yer boys to hold their fire.'

'Toss your weapons out!' ordered Jonas curtly. 'And keep them mitts high where I can see 'em.'

The revolver spiralled through the air as the rustler slowly, cautiously, emerged from cover. He was a big critter, a full head taller than Jonas, and broad as an ox. The red hair and beard were both straggly and matted, his range garb scuffed and worn. Red Chandler was not a pretty sight, in stark contrast to the shiny new Colt .44 Frontier that glinted in the sunlight.

The rest of the posse, what was left of them, charily approached the lone survivor of the deadly showdown.

Windy Rivers picked up the revolver and hefted it admiringly in his right hand. 'A mighty fine pistol,' he averred checking the load. 'Where'd yuh get it, mister?'

Chandler sniggered. 'The last owner suddenly found that he had no further use for it.'

'And neither have you,' Rivers snarled lunging at the rustler and slamming a bunched fist into the grinning maw. 'That's for shootin' down an unarmed man,' he spat.

Blood spouted from a bust nose as the startled

outlaw went down under the vicious onslaught. The bronc rider was all for continuing the assault when Jonas stayed his hand.

'That's enough!' he rapped out. 'The law will make sure that this jigger pays the the price for his owl-hooter ways.'

Red Chandler was quickly tied up.

Kansas Pete furtively circled around the pinioned rustler, curiously ogling him like he would some weird exhibit in a freak show. This was the first time the young livery man had ever seen a real live outlaw. He'd witnessed a few dead ones that had been brought in by the county sheriff back in his home town of Abilene, Kansas, but a living, breathing specimen was something else.

Chandler noticed the youngster's intrusive interest. The chance for a bit of innocent horseplay offered itself to his warped brain. Suddenly without any warning, he emitted a rabid growl. Baccy-stained teeth gnashed in truculent fury.

Pete staggered back, fear etched across his blanching features. He tripped over a saddle and went sprawling on to his back.

'Seen a ghost, kid?' howled the rustler, thoroughly delighted at the result of his prank.

Pete mumbled a vague imprecation as he scrambled to his feet, before slinking away to hide his embarrassment. His retreating back was followed by a few sly grins.

But the blacksmith had a more pressing issue on his mind.

'What about the reward he was talkin' about?' he enquired of the marshal. 'Do we get a share of it?'

Jonas considered the idea.

'Don't see why not. Equal shares for all.'

'How much is a hoss-thief worth these days?' scoffed Windy Rivers thrusting his bony face at the rustler.

Chandler drew himself up. He wiped a smear of blood from his mashed proboscis, mocking eyes casually surveying his captors. 'A deal more'n you turkeys'll ever make.' He accorded them a contemptuous smirk. 'How does an even grand suit?' Eyes lit up at the thought of all that dough. 'And don't be forgettin',' Chandler pointed out, nodding his head in the marshal's direction, 'starpackers don't merit any dividend when it comes to the payout of bounty.'

Jonas aimed a bitter scowl at the rustler's smug visage. It was he who now felt like sinking a bunched fist into the bastard's sneering mug. With the greatest effort, he managed to resist the temptation by moving away and checking that the stolen mustangs were securely penned into their stockade. Rivers had said that he and a couple of hands would come back and return them to the Summers ranch the following day.

Yet again the reason for his adopting this bogus persona had elbowed to the fore. After due consideration Jonas was able to console himself with the huge payday he was planning for the Clovis Gang in the not too distant future. That would sure wipe the smile off their faces.

After the dead bodies had been tied over the saddles of their mounts, it was a sombre yet jauntily sanguine posse that set off back down the valley. Windy Rivers led the way in single file. Even Kansas Pete had perked up at the thought of the fine stallion he would purchase with his share of the reward money.

NINE

FACE FROM
THE PAST

After consulting the old bronc rider, Jonas decided to take a more direct route across country back to Hashknife. He was anxious to reach town without delay to see if the new lawman had arrived. Should that disturbing state of affairs have come to pass, he would have a lot of awkward questions to answer. Not only that, he wanted to avoid a confrontation at the Summers Ranch. Old Buck might take it into his head to dole out his own form of vigilante justice against Red Chandler.

Rivers left the posse once they emerged from the constricting ravine of Redrock Alley. He promised to acquaint Buck Summers and his daughter with the results of their pursuit. The rancher's testimony would surely help put the rustler away for some considerable time.

It was late afternoon when the posse finally reached Hashknife. All their previous euphoria had dissipated due to the marshal's relentless pace. He had refused to call a halt in order to avoid another night camp. Any man who wanted to stretch his legs or attend to a call of nature had to catch up in his own good time.

Jogging down Main Street, the dust-caked posse had only one thing on their minds – a foaming tankard of cold beer at the Silver Wheel.

But at least they had not returned empty-handed.

Even Red Chandler had ceased his needling of the marshal. Indeed, he had become somewhat withdrawn, casting shady glances in the lawman's direction. On two occasions, Jonas had caught the man glaring at him, his ugly puss pinched and reflective.

The marshal was worried.

The notion that this turkey might have fingered him was niggling at his craw like a vexatious mosquito.

Jonas cast his mind back, racking his brains to determine whether their paths had crossed at some point in the past. But he kept drawing a blank.

Once he had delivered the bodies of the dead men to the undertaker, Jonas quickly hustled his prisoner into the jailhouse.

Having locked him up, his first job was to rifle through the stack of Wanted posters in search of any reference to Red Chandler. He finally located it at the bottom of the pile. And the rustler's growing assertion had erred on the side of caution: his bounty was a grand if brought in dead, but fifteen hundred alive.

With careful deliberation, he read through the description of all the outlaw's villainous activities. Chandler was wanted in three states for murder and extortion as well as rustling. But, try as he might, he just could not recall having met the guy.

His solemn thoughts were interrupted by a harsh bellow emanating from the cellblock.

'Hey, Marshal!' The gruff summons sounded almost like a choked guffaw. 'You in there . . . Marshal?' A mordant emphasis was laid on the lawman's title. 'I'm thinkin' that you and me have important issues to discuss.'

Jonas stiffened. He tipped a liberal measure of whiskey down his throat. Were these so-called *important issues* what he feared they were? He was in a quandary as to how this dilemma should be handled. If Red Chandler had recognized him, the guy was a visible and dangerous threat to all his plans.

'No use hidin' in there, Marshal,' iterated Chandler in a cocky tone of voice. 'Or should I say Mr Jim Kane?'

That did it. If the skunk started hollering out his outlaw name from the cell window, somebody was bound to hear and that would really upset the apple cart. Jonas leapt from his chair and quickly hurried through to the cellblock.

'What's all this racket?' he snapped. 'You want I should stick a gag round that big mouth?'

Chandler laughed. It emerged as a brittle roar.

'That would suit you just fine now, wouldn't it, Mr Kane?'

'Shut up, damn you,' interjected Jonas balling his fists while fearfully casting a wary eye towards the street. 'D'you want the whole blasted town to hear you spouting off?'

'Then you better start being more accommodatin' else that's exactly what I'll do.'

Jonas quickly shrugged off the stunning revelation that somehow this critter knew him from some place.

'So what makes you think my name is Jim Kane?' he asked.

'Yuh don't recognize me, do yuh?' Chandler got off his bunk and stepped up to the bars of the cell door. 'Take a closer look, Kane. Imagine me without all this hair and clean shaven.' Chandler smirked while striking a nonchalant pose. 'Difficult, I'll give yuh that.' Then his black eyes hardened to chips of ice. 'Now think back to a bank job in Springfield, Missouri. It was the spring of '66 just after the war.'

The red beard parted in a wide grin as the marshal struggled to bring the incident to mind.

He eyed the rustler closely before replying.

'OK, so I remember Springfield.' The admission was flat and devoid of expression. 'But I don't remember you being there.'

After the war, Jim Kane had joined forces with Wild Jack Dupree and the Missouri Jayhawkers. Like many others who found their war to be a big adventure, the Jayhawkers were loath to abandon the swashbuckling lifestyle they had enjoyed once peace was declared. Continuation of their lawless activities seemed like a natural progression. And an exceedingly profitable one as well.

Kane was only with the Jayhawkers for that one raid. They got away with over $5,000 but Dupree was shot in the process.

'You were the one who pulled Wild Jack out of that bank after he'd been plugged. Shot your way out of town like a man possessed, with him slung over your saddle. You were lucky not to get hit yourself with all that lead flyin' about.' Chandler stared hard at his old sidekick. There was more than a hint of respect in his measured delivery. 'But it was no use, was it? Old Jack died of his wounds. Soon after that the gang split up and we all went our separate ways.'

The rustler paused to allow the import of his disclosures to sink in.

'I was the one who shot the bank manager after he'd pulled that derringer hidden in his boot and drilled the boss.' Chandler's strident voice held a note of desperation. 'Do yuh remember now?'

It all came flooding back.

'Yeah! I recall now,' replied Jonas. 'But you weren't called Red Chandler then.'

The rustler shrugged. 'Changed my name, my appearance.' He tugged at his bushy red beard. 'The South was beat, and the Pinkertons were catchin' up with all the gangs. So I lit out from Missouri and headed West. New start, new opportunites. And this is one opportunity that you're gonna help me with.' Chandler laid a probing eye on the jittery bogus marshal, prodding a finger at the tin star. 'I don't give a damn why you've changed sides. But I'm durned sure the good citizens of this town would be mighty interested to learn that their trusted lawdog is naught but a common road agent.'

Spewing out a stream of lurid epithets that would

87

have seen a soldier blushing, Jonas grabbed his revolver and thumbed back the hammer.

'I could plug you here and now,' he stormed, jabbing the pistol's blued snout at the rustler. 'Claim you was shot while trying to escape.'

Chandler stood his ground unfazed.

'In minutes you'd have the whole town buzzin' around here to see what the ruckus was all about. They ain't gonna be too impressed to find a dead body still locked up.' His mocking disregard challenged Kane to find an alternative solution. 'And don't be thinkin' you could shift the body in time.' Chandler drew himself up to emphasize his bulky mass.

The marshal took a step back, the revolver lowering.

'So what d'you suggest,' he posed, in a less than confident tone.

Chandler's face split in a ghastly smile. He appeared to have it all worked out.

'Glad you've seen sense. The best way is to allow me to escape by leaving the cell door open,' he propounded briskly, secure in the knowledge that his plan would work. 'Bring my horse round to the back door, then you head off up town aways. Just so's I can see you through the window.' A twisted sneer had replaced the jaunty air. 'Don't want you double-crossin' me now, do I?' He paused for the import of his proposal to sink in. 'And leave a gun on the back step.'

'And how am I supposed to explain your sudden departure?' asked the sceptical starpacker.

Chandler shrugged. 'That's your business,' he shot back indifferently. 'I'm sure you'll think of somethin'.'

'I need time to think on it,' muttered Jonas. 'Figure out all the angles.'

'Well, don't take too long,' rasped Chandler, infecting a brittle edge to the remark. 'I've gotten a mighty short fuse.'

Lost in thought, Jonas returned to the office. He needed another drink to steady his nerves. This sudden resurrection ot his past and the threat it posed to his future was unnerving. He had got himself into a right muddle playing this dual role of desperado and starpacker. And it was frazzling his brains.

Why did life have to be so complicated? One day he was an outlaw planning a big robbery, the next a respected lawman. And now it was all under threat.

A rap on the outer door jerked his mind back to the present. The abrupt noise made him jump. Every knock could herald the arrival of the unwanted new marshal. The sooner this business was finished the better.

Sitting on the fence was no fun anymore.

'Who's there?' he called, a hand resting on the butt of his Peacemaker.

'Only me,' announced Molly Haskins brightly. 'Thought you and the prisoner could use a bite to eat.'

Jonas relaxed noticeably.

'Come in,' he replied, quickly secreting the bottle in his desk.

The grub smelled appetizing and reminded Jonas that, apart from the odd chaw on a stick of beef jerky, he had not eaten since the previous day.

'I could sure use this,' he beamed, taking up the knife and fork. 'Anything unusual happen in town while I was away chasing after them rustlers?' he asked, while spearing a chunk of beef.

'Nothing of any consequence,' murmured the girl thoughtfully.

But Jonas could sense a muted hesitance. His fork hung suspended in mid air. 'Something on your mind, Molly?' he enquired, warily.

'It's just that . . . well there's four men over at the diner now.'

'What about them?'

'Suspicious bunch of critters if'n you ask me,' she said.

Four men, suspicious!

Jonas was all ears.

'Describe them!' he snapped, then instantly regretted the brusque outburst. 'Sorry about that, Molly,' he hurried on, trying to allay the girl's startled reaction, 'but any shady characters who happen along need to be investigated with all this silver that's being lodged in the bank.'

'Of course, Marshal,' smiled Molly, suitably appeased. 'The leader was a shifty looking dude with curly black hair. He was with a small Mexican and a burly tough who was a touch on the simple side.'

'And the fourth man?'

'He arrived after the others. A cocky young kid with a limp.'

The Clovis Gang, it had to be!

They had arrived earlier than expected. But in view

of recent developments, perhaps that was no bad thing.

'Erm!' mused Jonas, apparently mulling over this informaton. 'Can't say I recognize the descriptions from the Wanted list. But I'll give them the once over after I've finished this hearty feast you've kindly brought.'

'Dont forget the prisoner,' chided Molly gently, as she moved to the door.

Jonas merely grunted. He had no intention of feeding Red Chandler. The bastard could starve for all he cared.

Gobbling down the food, Jonas gingerly opened the door and scanned the length of the street in both directions. It was early evening. Long shadows crept catlike down the dusty thoroughfare as the setting sun bathed the land in pink and gold striations.

Most of the mercantiles had closed up for the night. Few people were about which suited his purpose admirably.

Keeping well into the shadows, he flitted silently down the street. His intention was to catch the gang when they emerged from the Glad Tidings Diner and arrange a conflab away from any prying eyes and ears.

He slid into position around the side of the diner and waited. Building a smoke, he lit up and allowed the tobacco to do its duty, thankful that nobody passed by.

After ten minutes the door of the eating-house opened and Curly Ben stepped out on to the boardwalk. He slapped his bulging torso and belched loudly in appreciation of an enjoyable meal.

Jonas pursed his lips and hissed.

The gang boss tensed at the unfamiliar sound.

'Over here, Curly,' whispered Jonas gesturing for the emerging figures to join him in the alley which was now shrouded in a propitious blanket of gloom.

Clovis immediately recognized his lieutenant and quickly joined him along with the others. He was not slow in spotting the despised badge of office pinned to the marshal's leather vest.

'What's this fer?' he demanded harshly. 'You ain't joined the opposition, I hope?'

Jonas vehemently shook his head. 'It's a long story, boss,' he replied, urging the gang further down the alley to avoid any attention from nosey passers-by, 'Where you boys camped?'

'We've pitched out in a draw five miles east of here behind a rock pinnacle,' said Clovis. Jonas knew it well. Locals called it the Navajo Needle. But the gang leader's mind was on other issues as he pressed onward with his main concern. 'Have you figured out how we're gonna lift the silver shipment from here?'

'Can't discuss that sort of business now,' Jonas replied. 'It's too dangerous us being seen together. I'll ride out to your camp in two hours after I've done my rounds and the town's settled down for the night.'

'You certain this tinstar business ain't gone to your head?' prodded the Dakota Kid. 'It sits a bit too easy on yer vest fer my likin'.'

Jonas ignored the caustic rejoinder.

'Two hours,' he said, firmness etched across the

craggy demeanour. A last steady regard passed between outlaws and their foxy sidekick as he drifted away, swallowed by the gathering murk.

Back in the jailhouse, he was greeted by the prisoner baying for some positive response to his proposition. Chandler was becoming increasingly loud-mouthed and threatening, obliging Jonas to hurry into the cell-block.

'Cut that squawkin' if you wanna get out of here in one piece,' he rapped. 'This thing can't be hurried otherwise we'll both end up on Boot Hill. I'm workin' on how best to organize it so's I don't catch the blame.'

'Well hurry up about it,' grumbled Chandler impatiently, as he paced up and down the small cell. 'I ain't the most patient of guys.'

'So I'd noticed,' retorted Jonas acidly.

'And what about some grub? I'm starvin'.'

The marshal scowled. This varmint was getting too darned brazen.

'Comin' right up,' smirked the jailer returning to the office, a wily glint in his eye. He picked up the discarded supper tray delivered by Molly Haskins and hawked a lump of phlegm on to the plate. Then he carried it into the cellblock. With a quick flick of the wrist, he flung the congealed mess of cold left-overs at the startled prisoner.

'Enjoy your supper,' he guffawed, as Chandler howled with impotent wrath, the gluey remains splattered about his person.

TEN

A SHOCK FOR CURLY BEN

It was approaching midnight when Jim Kane, or Jonas Kelly as he was now known, finally slid out of Hashknife by a back route. He forked into the main trail after a mile to avoid being spotted. The last thing he wanted was some eagle-eyed citizen wondering what surreptitious business their new marshal could possibly be engaged in outside the town limits at such a late hour.

A crystal clear slice of moon bathed the undulating landscape in a spectral sheen. Vague rocky outlines assumed grotesque and fanciful shapes that might well have alarmed a less pragmatic individual. Trees became skeletal ogres reaching out with stick-thin limbs; boulders, hunched dwarves lying in ambush.

But the marshal had other things on his mind.

Curly Ben Clovis had questions. And Jim Kane had to supply the answers in order to secure a sizeable piece of the action.

In less than half an hour he sighted the narrow stack piercing the Stygian gloom ahead. Reining the sorrel down to a walk, he drew level with the Navajo Needle. As expected, a blurred figure emerged from behind a large boulder.

Chavez speared the approaching rider with a hard flinty glare, his rifle at the ready. On recognizing his sidekick, the Mexican pushed back his large sombrero and smiled. Nevertheless, he still adopted the cautious tactic that Curly Ben always insisted upon when the gang were camped out.

'Password!'

The sharp retort echoed back from the soaring bulk of the adjacent Needle. The visitor had expected it and responded with an equally curt rejoinder.

'Silver Dollar!'

The long barrel of the Springfield motioned the rider to pass.

'Good to see you again, Jim, my *amigo*,' trilled Chavez with a cheery wave. 'Camp ten-minute ride up draw around second bend. No chance of fire being seen from main trail.'

'Curly Ben always was a wary dude.'

'Ees reason gang still on loose,' asserted the Mexican with fervour.

'Can't disagree with you there, Chavez,' concurred Kane, jigging his mount forward.

*

But for all the bogus marshal's supposed care to avoid detection, his departure from Hashknife had not gone unnoticed.

Hank Rogers had been out late delivering a new ploughshare to a local farmer. He had himself been about to enter the town by the back door, though not for any covert reason. Suspicious by nature, the blacksmith had quickly hidden behind a rocky outcrop when he perceived a rider leaving at that late hour. Observing that it was the marshal, he had put two and two together and somehow arrived at a total of five.

Something didn't quite add up here.

So Rogers decided to trail him. Keeping as far back as possible without losing sight of him in the near dark, the blacksmith eventually saw the other rider stop beside the surging landmark that was the Navajo Needle. After a brief pause, the lawman turned off the trail heading along a draw that Hank Rogers had never previously noticed.

After letting Jim Kane enter the draw, Chavez was about to settle himself down in the lee of a boulder when a movement caught his eye. Instantly he was on the alert. Only one man had been expected.

So who was this nosy *molestia*?

Chavez discarded his rifle in favour of the trusted Bowie knife. He waited as the intruder approached. Then, knife arm raised in readiness, he called out in a low yet clear voice.

'Password!'

The man stiffened in the saddle.

'Who's there?' he demanded, his hand reaching

down to remove a rifle from its leather scabbard. 'Is that you, Marshal? What in thunder are you doing out here?'

A throaty growl bit the air as the Mexican launched his lethal missile.

Rogers never knew what struck him. No sound passed his lips as he slid from the saddle, dead before he hit the ground with a dull thud. Chavez waited a good five minutes to determine whether the intruder was alone. Satisfied that no other unwelcome guests were likely to emerge from the darkness, he snuck out from behind the cover of the rock and edged across to get a closer look at the man he had just killed.

He was a large guy to be sure. The leather apron and bulging muscles told the Mexican that he must have been the town blacksmith. No way could he move such a giant of a man on his own.

Chavez removed his sombero and scratched his head. He was flummoxed. The boss needed to be told about this and he was not going to be happy. Chavez responded with his characteristic shrug. What else could he have done? The guy was a threat who could have ruined all their plans. But leaving his post would mean the dead man being left out in the open.

Unaware of the fatal incident that had followed his entry into the draw, Jim Kane sat on a log sipping a mug of hot coffee.

Warily he eyed the hard faces staring back at him over the flickering embers of the camp-fire. The events that he had related about being mistaken for the new marshal of Hashknife needed some digesting.

And managing to hoodwink the townsfolk into believing he was the genuine article was received with sceptical grunts, especially from the Kid.

But Jim Kane had earned the full confidence of the gang boss, and that's what mattered as far as he was concerned.

'When d'yuh reckon will be the best time to hit the bank?' asked Clovis, anxious to bring the talk around to the reason for their being here.

'There's no chance of doing the bank,' asserted Kane firmly.

Clovis shot him a bleak look. 'Why not?' he snapped.

'Too well guarded. They have men posted round the clock.'

'What about when they move the silver to the refiner at Durango.'

Kane shook his head. 'It goes back with the monthly freight haulage wagons. And there's always at least five. Taking on the guards and drivers manning a train like that would be suicide.'

All these objections were getting on Curly Ben's nerves. Deep frown lines told Kane that his temper was threatening to erupt.

'So how the hell are we gonna pull it off?' Clovis snorted angrily.

'The best place is in Apache Pass while the silver is in transit from the Trujillo Mine.'

Kane paused to light up a cigar and, more importantly, to allow the frosty atmosphere to melt away. He handed one to Clovis who grudgingly accepted.

Satisfied that the gang boss was sufficiently thawed out, he then proceeded to outline the details.

'The wagon only has a driver and one guard riding shotgun. And once we've got the loot, I've discovered an old Indian trail that hasn't been used in over ten years. It'll make for the perfect getaway.'

For some minutes, Clovis considered the proposal. Finally he gave a nod of approval.

'You done well, Jim,' he commended, all his previous irritation forgotten. 'We'll meet up in town tomorrow in the saloon and go over the details.' Kane sighed as another fly in the ointment presented itself.

'I reckon it ain't in our best interests for you and the boys to be seen around town again,' he advised with pre-gauged caution.

'Why not?' hit back the Kid belligerently. 'Nobody's gonna tell me where I can and can't do my drinkin'.'

Kane stayed calm, keeping his response even and measured. 'Molly Haskins who runs the Glad Tidings Diner warned me that she thinks you're up to no good, reckons you're a bunch of desperadoes out to cause trouble.' A thin smile split his lips. 'That's not the sort of recommendation we want when planning to lift a silver shipment from under their noses.'

Clovis puffed out his chest. He was with the Kid when it came to deferring to the opinions of lesser mortals. But he was also astute enough to acknowledge that on this occasion, his lieutenant was right. They would need to remain out of sight.

Kane thought it best to omit that he had also earned the town's respect and had come to value this more than he had ever expected. Such an admission would not have been a healthy option. The Dakota Kid would have seen to that. Nor had he included any mention of Rachel Summers, particularly the emotional attachment he was uncomfortably aware was stirring in his breast.

Kane was not given any further oppotunity to struggle with his feelings. At that moment, the sound of shod hoofs echoing along the narrow draw found the desperadoes grabbing for their guns.

'It only me, boss,' called Chavez, from outside the tiny circle of light cast by the camp-fire.

'What in tarnation are you doin' here?' rasped Clovis acidly. 'You're meant to be on guard.'

'Man follow Jim from town,' gasped out the panting Mexican. 'He not give password.' Chavez paused, unsure how to deliver what he knew would be calamitous news.

'So what happened?'

The Mexican's swarthy features paled before Curly Ben's scathing retort.

'I had no choice,' he expostulated fearfully, ending with the baleful confession barely above a whisper. 'Had to kill heem.'

'With the knife?'

Chavez nodded expecting the worst. Curly Ben Clovis did not suffer setbacks gladly, however luckless.

A rabid growl bubbled up from deep within the gang-leader's throat.

But it never tasted the night air. It was Jim Kane who came to the Mexican's aid.

'The jasper must have seen me leave town and followed,' he admitted, setting himself between Clovis and the quaking Mex. 'Don't blame him, Ben. It was my fault for not taking enough care. I figured the whole goddamned town would have been asleep by that time.'

Clovis muttered under his breath but quickly simmered down. All the same, the news had shaken him.

'So how we gonna play this?' he demanded of his lieutenant.

'I figure if we hide the body in a ravine,' Kane proposed, 'nobody will be any the wiser. The guy just disappeared. Then after a few days, I can produce some of his clothes with tears and rips in them. Say I found 'em out in the bluffs. It'll appear as if a mountain cat's attacked him, then carried the carcass off to its lair.' He looked round at the grim faces struggling to absorb the import of all that had been said. 'There ain't no reason for them to dispute anything I tell 'em. So what d'you reckon?'

Nobody spoke as they mulled over the suggestion, all waiting for Curly Ben to give his verdict.

'Sounds good to me,' he announced at last with a grin. Turning to Chavez he rapped, 'You and Bulldog go get the body and bring it back here. We'll figure out where to hide it in the morning.'

Both Kane and the Mexican allowed themselves a quiet sigh of relief.

'I owe you one, *amigo*,' murmured Chavez quietly, as he got to his feet.

'There is one more thing,' added Kane, after the two outlaws had left.

The relaxed atmosphere instantly became distinctly frosty. Clovis and the Kid waited for Kane to continue.

'Got me a prisoner locked up in the town jail from that rustling operation I told you about.'

'So?'

'Waal!' Kane hesitated. 'He recognized me from a gang I used to run with after the war. The critter wants me to help him escape otherwise he'll blow the lid on my cover.'

'Hm,' muttered Clovis toeing a burning firebrand in thought. 'Seems like we've gotten a whole heap of problems tonight, ain't we?' Gritty peepers, hard as flint, held Kane in their powerful despotic grip. 'So who is this dude?' he asked tipping a hefty measure of whiskey into his coffee mug. With all that was going on, he reckoned he needed it.

'Goes by the name of Red Chandler,' replied Kane, trying to keep the waver out of his voice. Clovis had that effect on his associates. It was one reason nobody had ever challenged his leadership, even though he was no longer in his prime.

But Kane was unprepared for the jolting result that his remark had on the gang boss. On hearing the revelation, Clovis dropped his mug. The curly head snapped back as he leapt to his feet.

'Red Chandler, yer say?'

Kane nodded blankly, taken aback by this unexpected reaction.

'You know him, boss?' enquired the Kid.

'Darned right I know him.' The words emerged as a rancid snarl, flat and cold as frozen mutton. 'The bastard only killed my brother.' He hawked a globule of spittle into the fire watching it writhe and sizzle. 'Chandler shot him in the back after Dave had caught the rat cheatin' at cards. I swore on Dave's tombstone that I'd avenge him one day. And now's my chance.'

He punched the palm of his hand. The smile that creased Curly Ben's grizzled features was chilling to behold. Even the Dakota Kid blanched before the daunting gaze.

For the next half-hour, they discussed how best this could be achieved. Once it had been agreed, Kane bade them farewell and mounted up for the return to Hashknife. Secreted in his saddle-bag was the black-smith's leather apron, suitably clawed for the benefit of the town council of which Hank Rogers was, or had been, a prominent member.

They had agreed to meet up again the following night after the gang had bushwacked Red Chandler. Kane would then be able to claim the credit for bringing in the escaped outlaw, this time for an appointment with the undertaker.

ELEVEN

COLONEL MORTIMER FRANKS

'Time for you to disappear, Chandler,' announced the marshal unlocking the cell door. It was the following night. A pale moon filtered through the bars of the cell window providing sufficient light for the nefarious event about to be enacted. 'There's a horse out back with your holster and sixgun slung over the saddle horn.' He omitted to inform the outlaw that it was not loaded.

'About time as well,' grunted Chandler levering himself off the bunk.

'Take the trail heading east,' advised Kelly firmly. 'I'll tell the mayor that I reckon you've gone south hoping to get over the border into New Mexico. That'll give you a head start.'

'Good thinkin',' agreed Chandler, stepping into the

corridor. 'Maybe we'll meet up again sometime.'

'Don't think about coming back this way,' warned Kane acidly. 'Next time I won't be so accommodating.'

Chandler shrugged before posing a final inquisitive query. 'So how you gonna explain away the escape to the good citizens of Hashknife?'

The marshal produced a bent fork.

'I'll claim you kept this back from your dinner, then picked the lock and surprised me.'

The outlaw nodded. Then without warning he slammed a hard fist into the marshal's jaw. All of Red Chandler's more than ample weight was behind the solid blow. The sudden move caught the lawman completely unawares. Without a murmur he slumped to the floor, out cold.

'Well that's another surprise for you. Just to make it look real,' chortled the escapee following up with a brutal kick in the ribs. 'And that's for treatin' me like a rank bad smell.' Shreds of dried food still clung to the outlaw's grimy shirt. 'Next time we meet up, you're history, fella.'

Slipping out the back door, Chandler strapped on the gunbelt and mounted his horse. He cautiously nudged the bay gelding around the shadowy cluster of buildings heading in the direction of the Navajo Needle.

Ben Clovis had positioned his men on either side of the trail. The sky was clear with a myriad twinkling stars adding to the burnished radiance of the moon. The gang boss was confident they would experience no trouble in picking off the escaping outlaw.

But there were to be no killing shots.

'I want that skunk to know who it is that's diggin' his grave,' hissed Clovis planting himself behind a boulder overshadowed by the haunting sentinel of the Needle.

It was a further half-hour before the measured tread of trotting hoofs reached their ears. Hands tightened around rifle stocks. With keen eyes squinting in the ethereal glow of the moon, the outlaws made ready for the ambush.

Five minutes later, a blurred shadow pierced the grey sky to the west. As the most proficient rifleman, Dakota had been nominated to bring the rider down with a well-placed glancing shot.

The harsh blast obliterated the silence. It was followed immediately by a stiffled cry as the rider tumbled from the saddle and lay writhing on the ground.

Clovis quickly emerged from cover and sprinted across to the bewildered figure who was already struggling to his feet. The bullet had lifted his hat and burned a thin furrow across his scalp. Blood oozed from the wound but it was not serious. A vicious backhander with the full force of Bulldog Maddox behind it felled the addled desperado.

An anguished groan issued from between split lips as Chandler struggled to understand what had befallen him. His head felt like it had been kicked by a loco mule. Fighting to stave off the waves of nausea that threatened to drag him under, Chandler shrank back under the bleak gaze of the four hard-nosed rannies gathered round.

But it was the desperate nature of his situation that soon dispelled the bleary-eyed torpor.

'Who are you fellas?' he muttered, fearfully appraising his captors. 'I ain't got a thing that's worth the robbin',' he pleaded. 'Only just escaped from the jail in Hashknife. You've bushwacked the wrong guy.'

'Your name Red Chandler?'

The rustler turned towards the speaker. A grim expression devoid of any pity glowered down at him.

'H-how d'yuh kn-know my name?' stammered the outlaw. 'I never set eyes on you afore.'

'Maybe so,' spat Clovis bending low and grabbing the jigger by his shirt front. A button popped revealing a bobbing Adam's apple. 'But you know my brother cos it was you who shot him.'

'Who are yuh then?' mumbled Chandler, mesmerized by the macabre glare.

Clovis jammed his revolver into the quivering snout of his victim.

'The name's Clovis,' he rasped. 'Curly Ben Clovis.'

Chandler's eyes widened at the mention of the infamous desperado's name.

'And my brother went under the handle of Solitaire Dave. You claimed he was cheatin' at cards. But Dave was a good poker player, one of the best. He had no need to operate a rigged game. . . . Remember now?'

The blood drained from Chandler's leathery features. He recalled the game vividly.

'But it was all a big mistake,' maintained Chandler, desperation evident in his croaking appeal. 'My gun

107

went off accidentally and Dave just happened to be in the way.'

'Well, now you're in the way,' glowered Clovis, 'of my revolver.'

Slowly he rose to his feet, stepped back a pace and aimed his pistol at the squirming killer. A lurid grin devoid of all humour settled across the saturnine countenance. The click of the hammer racking back to full cock sounded all the more poignant in the still air of the night.

'And this ain't no accident.' The smile had slid from his face the judgement delivered in a frigidly joyless monotone.

Two shots drove the hapless outlaw into the ground as the executioner carried out his avowed declaration of vengeance. It had been festering inside his soul for five long years. Curly Ben felt as if a huge weight had been lifted from his shoulders.

He turned away.

'Make sure that piece of trash is left in a prominent position for Jim to find when he rides out this way in the morning,' he ordered.

'You in there, Marshal?'

It was the strident voice of Molly Haskins. After receiving no response to her knocks on the outside door of the office, she had entered to find the place empty. Already eight in the morning, she would have expected the lawman to be up and about by this time.

A muffled groan from the cell block found her hustling through just as the lawman was trying to regain his feet. His legs were shaky and weak. Dried blood caked his head where it had struck the side of the iron bunk when he fell. And an ugly lump the size of a duck egg was already visible beneath the dishevelled mass of blond hair. Gingerly he felt the swollen jaw. Tender and sore to the touch, at least it wasn't broken.

Setting the breakfast tray down, Molly quickly helped the injured man up on to the bunk. Then she dribbled some water down his parched throat.

'What happened, Marshal?' she asked. Peering about, she suddenly realized that Red Chandler was no longer in residence. A dark frown creased her florid countenance. 'And where's the prisoner?'

Molly's puzzled query met with another anguished croak before the marshal was able to respond. He shook his head in an attempt to dispel the cobwebs ensnaring his addled brain. A cup of strong hot coffee acted as a further restorative.

He now felt sufficiently coherent to play the hand he had dealt himself regarding the fake escape. And resume his role as Jonas Kelly – US marshal.

'The varmint overpowered me when I came in to refill his water bottle. Only turned my back for a second and he jumped me.' The bent fork was conveniently in view on the floor which Jonas now pointed to. 'He must have picked the lock, then slugged me hard and lit out the back way.' Jonas dragged himself to his feet. 'He'll have a good five hours' start. So I'd better get after him pronto.'

Molly eased him back down on to the bunk. Still

concussed and suffering from shock, she realized that first and foremost he needed the services of the doctor.

'You ain't going no place, Marshal, until the doc's given you the OK.' Her firm businesslike tone brooked no rebuttal, and Jonas allowed the café owner to take control. The slow smile playing lightly across his bruised features caused a pained wince. Things could not be working out better.

After prescribing some ointment for his jaw and a cold compress for the head injury, Doc Logan assured the patient that he would be good as new in a few days' time. Just to take things easy in the meantime. There was little chance of that in view of the body awaiting collection at the Navajo Needle.

Once the doctor had left, a liberal slug of whiskey helped numb the aches and pains, making him feel more like his old self.

That's when a babble of voices out in the street caught his attention. Hurrying outside he was met by the Clovis Gang trundling down the middle of the thoroughfare as calm as you please. And behind Bull Maddox, was the body of the escaped rustler draped across the saddle of his cayuse.

Jonas's lower jaw hung open in dismay. What in tarnation was Clovis thinking of coming into town as bold as brass like this? The guy had brushed aside his warning to keep a low profile. Now the fat would really be in the fire.

Spotting the marshal ogling them, Clovis guided his mount over to the hitching rail in front of the jail-house.

Without preamble he addressed the gaping lawman in a brisk, self-assured tone, sufficiently loud for all the watching citizens to hear.

'Good morning, Marshal,' he breezed, doffing his hat. The greasy black curls glinted in the morning sunlight. 'Colonel Mortimer Franks at your service, sir.'

Jonas was nonplussed, lost for words.

So Clovis carried on, unabashed by his henchman's bewilderment. By this time, the strange gathering had reached the ears of the mayor, who bustled along the sidewalk from his office in the company of Cranford Jagger, the bank manager.

'I've only just heard that our prisoner has escaped,' voiced the mayor queasily eyeing the corpse. Then in a more supercilious vein added, 'Perhaps you would he good enough to explain what happened, Mister—?'

'Franks, Colonel Mortimer Franks,' smiled the gang leader affecting an unctious tone. 'My associates and I are in the area to look over the prospect of setting up a mining operation. We heard in Denver that a new silver strike has been made in Conejos County.'

'You are certainly correct in that assumption, sir,' deemed Flockhart loftily. 'Your business here would be more than welcome. Isn't that so, Mr Jagger?'

The banker bobbed his head, rapacious beady peepers gleaming with anticipation at the thought of a big time Denver businessman pouring greenbacks into the town.

Having recovered his composure, Jonas stood back admiring his partner's gall. Ben Clovis certainly had style. And he now had the town council eating out of his hand. There was every prospect that the mayor would be hoodwinked enough to offer the gang free accommodation at the town's only hotel.

'This fellow stumbled upon our camp out by the Navajo Needle. Being an observant judge of character, my partner here' – Clovis paused to sling a thumb at the Dakota Kid – 'reckoned he had seen the fellow's depiction on a Wanted poster. When challenged, the varmint went for his gun.' The Kid adopted a suitably grave demeanour. Clovis shrugged his shoulders raising both hands to indicate his chagrin at the terminal results of the confrontation. 'We had no choice but to defend ourselves.'

'Of course, of course,' concurred the mayor, indicating for some of the onlookers to carry the body down to the undertaker's parlour. Seth Torbin was already measuring up the corpse. Then he returned to the subject that was much closer to his heart. 'Any information you require concerning available prospecting sites, do not hesitate to call at my office.'

Flockhart rubbed his hands with grasping anticipation. 'There will, of course, be a share of the reward money forthcoming,' he said.

Clovis dismissed the offer with a shake of his head. 'We are only too pleased to deliver up such an notorious brigand into the hands of the law.' A humorous smirk was levelled at Jonas Kelly.

Bulldog Maddox could only goggle open-mouthed. He had never seen the gang boss in this vein before. And openly refusing a reward! The Kid stiffened in

112

the saddle, struggling to remain dispassionate. Refusing easy money was anathema to his covetous heart.

Clovis himself was enjoying the situation. And Jonas could barely maintain a straight face. The whole thing was akin to a theatrical play.

'And now if you could point us in the direction of the nearest hostelry,' concluded the gang leader swinging his horse round, 'my partners and I are in need of liquid refreshment.'

'Right across the street, gentlemen,' interjected Cranford Jagger. Then, to Clancy the bartender, 'Anything these gentlemen want is on the town, including accommodation until they find something of a more permanent nature.'

'Your generosity will be rewarded in Heaven,' said Clovis in a smarmy voice. His men were already jigging their mounts towards the Silver Wheel.

Jonas shook his head in wonderment as he joined them.

Now that the fun was over, there was serious business to discuss.

'It will be my pleasure to show these er . . . gentlemen around,' he said to allay any curious notions.

'One more thing,' called Flockhart after the marshal's retreating back. 'Have you by any chance seen Hank Rogers during your forays into the surrounding countryside?'

Jonas accorded him a suitably puzzled frown.

'He hasn't been seen for a couple of days,' continued the mayor. 'And according to his wife, he should have been home around midnight on Monday after delivering a new plough share to Josh Carter over San Pedro way.'

Jonas considered the question before shaking his head.

'Can't say that I have,' he replied thoughtfully, noting the slight lift of the eyebrows from the Colonel. 'I'll take a ride out that way once I've got these gentlemen settled in.'

TWELVE

GREEN-EYED MONSTER

Clovis headed for a table in the far corner of the saloon where no twitchy ears could listen in. He engaged in idle chatter until Clancy had set down a bottle of Blue Label imported Scotch whisky together with five glasses.

'That's the finest liquor this side of the Mississippi,' crowed the bartender.

Clovis hooked out the cork and poured himself a generous measure.

'Your very good health, sir,' he declared brightly, raising the glass. 'Now if you wouldn't mind, we have serious matters to discuss with the marshal.'

'Certainly, gentlemen,' pledged the barman backing away. 'I will make sure you are not disturbed.'

Once they had been left alone, Clovis instantly

dropped the assumed persona resuming his more imperious mien.

Addressing Jim Kane he snapped, 'So what's the plan of action gonna be?'

Kane peered around before replying. Following an initial interest occasioned by the arrival of Red Chandler's corpse, nobody was paying them any further heed. The low murmur of innocuous jabbering from the other patrons helped to muffle their own clandestine talk.

'We're in luck,' announced Kane, lowering his voice. The others huddled round to hear what he had to say. 'The next delivery of silver from the Trujillo Mine is due on Friday. That gives you a full day to make yourselves familiar with the terrain around Apache Pass.'

'How do we find it?' asked Maddox.

Chavez cut in with a lilting assurance that he knew the place from his last fleeting visit to Hashknife.

'Six maybe seven miles west out of town ees fork in zee trail,' explained the Mexican, 'Left to Durango right for bluffs and Apache Pass. It ees only route through to mine on far side.' Then he shook his head. 'But Chavez not been through.'

'Ride out there tomorrow,' suggested Kane. 'After all, you're potential silver prospectors looking for a likely place to set up. So it won't cause any wagging tongues if anyone sees you over that way. Then you can figure out the best place for the hold-up.'

'Sounds good,' agreed Clovis, his eyes burning with fiery anticipation.

'What about you?' rasped the Kid aiming a bleak look at the bogus lawman. 'What you gonna be doin' while we're riskin' our hides?'

Kane emitted an irked sigh while trying to keep a lid on his temper. He could see that at some point soon there was going to be a showdown with this cocky sidewinder. Until then, he would need to maintain a cool head.

So he ignored the blunt interruption.

'Once the silver has been lifted, you will need to hide out at Pueblo Bonito until everybody figures you've left the territory. I'll raise a posse and lead them on a wild goose chase in the opposite direction. I suggest we give it a week. Then I'll join you and we'll take the old Indian trail over the mountains into New Mexico.'

Once he had finished, Kane waited for the gang boss to digest the plan. Clovis slowly sipped the prime single malt, his gaze fixed and remote. For two minutes nobody spoke, nor moved a muscle. All four henchman sat tense and expectant, waiting on their leader's decision.

Finally, Clovis set his empty glass down. A smile cracked open the leaden façade.

'Fill 'em up, Bulldog,' he ordered breezily. Once the burly outlaw had complied, Clovis again raised his glass. 'To a successful job . . . *gentlemen!*'

The last word was uttered in an exaggerated inflection which helped ease the tight atmosphere of seconds before.

*

Ten minutes later, once again in the guise of Jonas Kelly, the marshal was back in his office. He was preparing to ride out in search of the 'missing' blacksmith when the door opened and Rachel Summers came in.

The girl had taken special care with her appearance, a fact that was not lost on the ogling lawman who hastily removed his hat. The appearance of the Clovis Gang had temporarily removed the winsome girl from his thoughts. That omission was now vigorously rectified.

Momentarily he was lost for words. Lawless images of the silver hold-up jarred with amatory feelings of which he had little experience. The two conflicting visions left his nerves frayed and cranky.

Rachel did not appear to have noticed the marshal's dilemma.

'I've left Pa in the capable hands of Dr Logan,' she said, 'His wounds are mending fine, but the doc needs to give him the all clear.' Jonas gaped at her, merely nodding inanely as she carried on unawares. 'So I thought we might have lunch together. Molly Haskins has a special on today. And then you can tell me all about this strange gentleman everybody's talking about. The one who brought in the body of the escaped prisoner.'

Mention of Red Chandler's demise brought Jonas back down to earth with a bump. The last thing he wanted was to discuss those highly charged events. And especially not the sudden appearance of *Colonel Mortimer Franks.*

118

That very same personage now appeared as a dubious saviour in the doorway of the office. The gang boss hustled in without knocking. He was just about to pose a question regarding the forthcoming hold-up when he noticed the comely female hovering to one side.

With consummate ease, he slipped back into the guise of a Civil War veteran.

Curly Ben had always prided himself on being a lady's man. Not for him the sordid tumblings associated with soiled doves, Clovis had always sought out the allure of a more sophisticated breed of woman. It was the challenge that he enjoyed as much as the conquest.

And he recognized instantly that Rachel Summers was just such an example. His eyes glittered in keeping with the oily smile.

'Are you not going to introduce me to your friend, Marshal?' he murmured with effortless charm.

Jim Kane knew all about his leader's reputation in that arena. His hackles rose as he made the introductions, quickly remembering to assume his part in the spurious affair. As the two conversed, Curly Ben self-assured as his hypnotic attraction took control, Jonas sensed the green-eyed monster twisting his heart-strings.

Another saviour now came to his aid, this time in the solid dependence of Dr Logan. The firm knock on the door never came at a more propitious moment.

'Come in!' shouted the relieved lawman.

The spider's web was broken as the medic entered.

119

'Your father is fine, Rachel,' he said, according the deflated Clovis a curt nod. 'All he needs is to rest up for a few days and that leg will be good as new. But no horse riding for at least another week.'

'Don't worry, I'll make sure he toes the line,' she concurred.

'He also wants you to meet him in the general store in five minutes,' the medic added with a chuckle as he was leaving. 'I wouldn't keep that old guy waiting. He can get mighty tetchy when he ain't in the driving seat.'

'Much obliged, Doc.' Rachel smiled knowingly whilst securing her bonnet. After wrapping a shawl around her slim shoulders, she made to follow the doctor outside.

'Nice to make your acquaintance, Colonel Franks,' she smiled, offering him a coquettish bow. 'Perhaps we will met again sometime.'

'The pleasure will be all mine, Miss Summers,' he drooled.

But Clovis knew there would be no further meeting. He was merely playing a game. Nonetheless, he had quickly perceived Jim Kane's reaction to his charm. And he found it disturbing. What other distractions had affected the guy's ability to service the gang's ambitions? Had the Kid been right after all in voicing his distrust?

'You'd be well advised not to get too close to that dame, Jim,' propounded Clovis in a sombre tone. 'She ain't for the likes of you and me.'

Kane shrugged indifferently.

'Don't know what you mean,' he snapped, with a little too much bite.

Clovis chose not to pursue the matter.

'Just sayin' is all. We got a job to do, then its *adios* Colorado.' He fastened a baleful eye on to his sidekick. 'And I trust you to play your part. Savvy?'

'Don't you fret none, Ben,' he replied with rock-solid assurance. 'You boys can count on me.'

After discussing some salient points regarding the timing of the hold-up, Clovis left. Nothing more was intimated regarding Kane's potential for treachery. The gang leader was confident that his lieutenant would do what was expected.

Jim Kane was not so certain.

THIRTEEN

APACHE PASS

Clovis arranged for each of his men to slip out of Hashknife separately on the day of the silver shipment. He did not want to advertise the fact that four strangers were heading in the direction of Apache Pass. He figured they would be prime suspects once the robbery had been reported. But there was no sense in heedlessly raising suspicions. Like as not there were other critters in town with noses longer than that of the blacksmith.

They had chosen a place in the middle section of the pass at its narrowest point. Here the trail swung round in a dog-leg which would force the wagon down to walking pace. Massive boulders on either side offered more than enough cover from which to neutralize any attempted resistance on the part of the guards.

Clovis had made certain of arriving early. Kane had

assured him that the shipment did not leave the Trujillo Mine before mid-morning. That meant it should arrive at the point of ambush around noon. But Clovis was not taking any chances.

He looked at his timepiece. It read 10.30 a.m.

Already the sun was beating down with a fiercesome heat. Hemmed into the towering cliffs of fractured rock only served to increase the sun's intensity. Overhead the ceiling of virginal blue was unbesmirched by any sign of a cloud. And within the confines of the pass, dust devils egged on by the over-heated air weaved and cavorted between the rocky outcrops.

The heat was affecting them all. But it was always Bulldog Maddox who suffered most due to his exces-sive hulk. Already he was tipping the contents of his water bottle down a parched gullet.

'Take it easy with that,' warned Clovis. 'You gotta make it last. There won't be no fill-ups until this job is done and we're well clear.'

The hefty bruiser grudgingly set the life-giving elixir aside. But as the minutes dragged by, his eyes increasingly veered that way. Clovis shrugged. It was his funeral, just so long as it was after they'd success-fully lifted the silver. Only Chavez appeared indiffer-ent, the large sombrero acting as a giant sun shade.

As the noon hour approached, the gang boss reminded his men of what needed to be done.

'Don't forget, boys,' he emphasized with vigour, 'we don't take no prisoners on this one,' which meant that neither of the guards would leave Apache Pass alive.

It was a departure from their normal method of robbery, but Clovis did not want any witnesses. He had assured Jim Kane that the haulage employees would be spared if they co-operated with the outlaws. However, because they needed to go to ground on Pueblo Bonita for a week until the hue and cry had died down, the more time they were accorded to achieve the disappearing act, the better. Most of all, he did not want any eagle-eyed guard imparting a detailed description of the bandits.

'Take your places,' he hissed, levering the Winchester purposefully, 'and make every shot count.'

Maddox and Chavez slipped across to the far side of the narrow ravine. Once in position, they each signalled to Clovis.

'Kane ain't gonna be too pleased about that, boss,' sneered Dakota, fingering his pistol with meaningful intent. The Kid would like nothing more than for the bogus starpacker to take umbrage. He had ambitions. And they included becoming a key player in this set up. Jim Kane was a boil that needed lancing. His flinty gaze locked on to that of the boss. 'But I can handle him.'

'Don't you worry none about Jim,' replied Clovis, 'He'll come around to my way of thinkin' once he sets his peepers on all that lovely loot.'

But the Kid was having none of it. Clovis was getting soft in his old age. Perhaps it was time for a younger man to take over this operation. He would bide his time and see how things panned out.

*

It was another half-hour before they heard the rumble of wagon wheels and shod hoofs drumming rhythmically on the hard-packed earth. A gentle whinny from the lead horses indicated that the driver had applied the brake as he approached the familiar obstacle of the dog-leg.

Rifle barrels poked out from behind rocks.

Curly Ben was always the one to start the ruckus. Anybody who elected to open fire before him would be in for a hard time once the dust had settled.

He waited until the team was at its slowest before letting rip.

Rifle fire tore the silence to shreds. Seconds later, hot lead was stabbing at the team of six and its heavily laden wagon. The initial volley of shots lifted the driver from his seat. The guy never knew what hit him. He tumbled over the side of the wagon, dead before he hit the ground.

The panic-stricken horses reared up. They were threatening to stampede down the ravine. Such an occurrence would have really upset the gang's carefully laid plans. Clovis realized that there was no alternative: he quickly pumped a couple of bullets into the heads of the two lead horses.

His rapid-fire aim was instinctive and true. The ruthless deed effectively brought the whole caboodle to a shuddering halt. Stumbling and dithering, the other horses tried desperately to push forward, unaware that their colleagues had met with an abrupt finale. But to no avail.

The guard inside the coach quickly recovered from

the surprise attack. He began laying down a barrage of concentrated fire at the two bushwackers on his right. But with two more on the opposite side of the trail, he stood little chance. The Kid took advantage of the unequal contest to shimmy down a loose gully. Bending low, he scuttled over to the open window of the big wagon and peered inside.

A pitiless smile of satisfaction spread itself across the malevolent visage. 'Over here, mister' he jipped gleefully. The startled guard swung his head to face this unexpected threat, bulging eyes agog with horror. 'Now say yer prayers.'

But the poor sap never got the chance. Three shots rang out forming a tiny triangle across the unfortunate jigger's heart. Blood pulsated from the ruptured organ.

Dakota blew smugly on the smoking barrel of his pistol.

'Now that's what I call good shootin',' he muttered to himself.

The Battle of Apache Pass had taken a little over one minute. An ominous silence descended on the grim scene along with the clouds of shifting sand. Tendrils of smoke from the discharged firearms floated with fluid ease on the hot thermals.

'OK, boys,' voiced Clovis, emerging from cover. 'We need to get the silver away from here pronto.' He called to Maddox who was leading their mounts out from the cover of a nearby chunk of rockface. 'Over here, Dog. Get these boxes loaded on to the mules, two either side. And, Chavez!'

126

'*Sí patrón?*'

'You make sure they're secured good and tight.'

The Kid stood to one side idly watching the transfer. His sullen features assumed a lurid grimace. Slowly and methodically he ejected the spent cartridges from his revolver before thumbing new ones into the chamber.

That was when an idea began to form in his twisted brain.

That lunkhead Maddox was heaving a strongbox up on to the crosstree saddle lashed to one of the mules. Chavez was concentrating on tying it down. And Clovis? A venomous glare speared the gang leader's back as he tended to his own weapons.

Quickly absorbing the scene, Dakota stiffened, his whole body tense and alert. Never again would he get a better opportunity than this. All that was needed were a couple of well-placed shots in the exposed back, and the silver would be his for the taking.

He could easily handle Maddox and the greaser. Neither was any kind of match for his gun arm.

As if in slow motion, so as not to draw attention to his treachery, the Kid drew his revolver and thumbed back the hammer. He aimed it purposefully at the clearly defined target, no more than fifteen feet away. Only a blind man could miss at that distance.

It was his undoing that Bulldog Maddox chose that moment to swivel his beady eyes towards the lounging Kid. Normally slow on the uptake, witnessing the terminal threat to his mentor's very existence propelled the lumbering outlaw's grey matter into overdrive.

'Behind you, boss!' he yelled.

Clovis might well have been past the first flush of youth, but his reflexes were instant and spontaneous. Throwing himself to the left, he spun just as the Kid fired. A burning sensation of hot lead scorched his hair line. But the sudden jolt of agony barely registered.

His lithe body twisted, the Peacemaker palmed and spitting a lethal reply of its own. Three shots merged into a single blast of deadly peril striking the stunned kid in the middle of his forehead. No tiny triangle here, just a single hole as the traitor lurched backwards, arms flailing wildly.

There was no need for any follow-up. The Dakota Kid's double-dealing perfidy had been brought to an ignominious and blunt end.

Clovis snarled at the twitching corpse.

'Get this sneakin' lowlife off the trail,' he rasped. The only hint that anything untoward had just occurred was the slight tic above his right eye. 'And make sure he's well out of sight.'

Slapping the trail dust from his duds, the gang leader replaced his hat firmly and aimed a gob of spittle at the splayed out traitor.

While Maddox was heaving the dead weight on to his broad shoulders, Curly Ben said quietly, 'That's earned you an extra bonus, Dog.'

The big outlaw smiled. 'Gee, thanks, boss. It weren't nothin'.'

Clovis replied with a sideways guffaw.

'Well it sure was to me.'

A yawning beam split the Bulldog's coarse visage.

Inside of fifteen minutes, the three horsemen were ready to leave the site of the brief yet deadly conflict. Their destination was the abandoned settlement of Pueblo Bonita.

But, much to Curly Ben's bewilderment, the supersitious Mexican insisted that the two dead silver hauliers should be accorded the dignity of a decent burial alongside the trail. He was forced to kick his heels while his two confederates set to work. Chavez even said a few words over their graves finishing with a sign of the cross.

'Are we ready to pull out now?' questioned the frustrated gang leader, impatiently studying his timepiece for the fifth time. His comment contained more than a whiff of irony, but the remark was totally lost on his confederate.

Chavez replied with a solemn nod. 'They innocent *obreros*, deserve proper send-off.'

Nevertheless, it was an upbeat party that pulled out of Apache Pass that Friday afternoon. Clovis took the vanguard leading the small train of four mules back down the gorge, Maddox and Chavez bringing up the rear. Three of them could easily handle the mules with their heavy burden of precious metal ore. And once Jim Kane joined them, they could light out for pastures new.

The Kid had never been popular with either Chavez or Maddox. He had only been brought in on account of his fast gun hand. Both men quickly concluded that he would not be missed.

'Never would have figured that skulkin' rat for a backshooter,' remarked Maddox to his sidekick.

The Mexican rolled his eyes, then spat in agreement. 'Him greedy *vibora*. Want all of loot for self. Such a *hombre* does not deserve proper burial.'

'Well, he sure was paid in full for his treachery.'

'You right there, big man,' agreed Chavez smiling.

'You fellas make sure to rub out our trail once we leave the pass,' Clovis reminded his confederates.

'We're on it, boss,' replied Maddox, trailing a spray of cottonwood behind them.

The marshal was strolling along the main street when the agitated figure of Cranford Jagger emerged from the bank. Spotting the marshal, he crossed the street at a run.

Breathing heavily from the unaccustomed exertion, he burbled, 'The silver hasn't arrived from Trujillo yet. It should have been here four hours ago.'

'Maybe they were late setting off,' suggested the lawman, trying to appear concerned. 'Could be any number of things.'

The bank manager was not convinced.

'This has never happened before,' he prattled, worry lines scoring deep furrows across his florid brow. 'I have a feeling that something bad's happened.'

'What d'you mean?'

'A robbery, that's what I mean,' snapped the

anxious banker. 'I reckon as the law around here, you should head out to the mine and see what's going on.'

Kelly hesitated. The more time he could delay things, the better for Curly Ben and the gang to hide the loot on Pueblo Bonita.

'Let's wait until tomorrow,' he said. 'If the silver wagon ain't arrived by then, I'll ride out that way and investigate. No point going off half-cocked when there might be some simple explanation.'

Jagger grumbled and muttered huffily before agreeing.

'I'll set off at first light,' iterated Kelly to the banker's retreating back. A half smile drifted across the granite features. And you can be sure that I'll do my darnedest to solve the mystery, he mused with a wry glint in his eye.

FOURTEEN

RIDE TO NOWHERE

The false dawn was hovering over the eastern horizon trying to usher in the new day when a lone rider galloped headlong down the main street of Hashknife. Even though the chill of early morn encased the landscape, the lathered cayuse was sweating profusely. The rider hauled back on the reins in front of the marshal's office. Everything was still in darkness. Not a light showed anywhere.

The tired rider hastened up to the office door and hammered on it fiercely using the butt of his pistol.

'Wake up, Marshal,' he hollered in a panicky voice.

The urgent summons brought the groggy lawman stumbling down the stairs from his rooms above the office.

'What's all this noise,' he demanded, opening the office door while fisting the grittiness of sleep from his eyes. 'Can't a fella get his fair share of shut-eye around here?'

The caller ignored the protest.

'The silver shipment's been taken,' he blurted out, stamping his boots in flustered agitation.

Wide awake now that he knew the fatal hold-up had been successfully undertaken, Jonas Kelly quickly slipped into the role of a concerned officer of the law. He applied a lighted taper to an oil lamp. The illumination caught the haunted eyes of a thin, gaunt jasper of indeterminate age.

'What evidence have you to back up this fantastic claim?' he challenged.

'The evidence of my own eyes, is all,' rasped the man, indignant at being made to explain himself. 'I was returning to the mine after checking the transit arrangements to Durango. Figured I'd make it back without a night camp and came across the wagon and two dead horses in Apache Pass. Shook me up, I can tell yuh.'

'And what about the silver?' asked Jonas.

'Gone!' rapped the man. 'Every last chunk. They even took the strongboxes.'

Jonas went back inside the office and strapped on his gunbelt, then walked over to the gun rack and selected a Winchester and two boxes of shells. By this time, the hullaballoo had attracted an audience. The mayor hustled across the street elbowing aside the crowd. He was followed by Cranford Jagger with a blanket draped over his night shirt.

'What did I tell you, Marshal?' grumbled the tetchy

banker. 'I knew the silver had been robbed.'

'You knew about this?' enquired Flockhart, eyeing the lawman dubiously.

'I told him last night but he didn't believe me,' intersected the edgy banker.

'Well, it appears you were right. I only wanted to make certain before rushing off on some wild goose chase,' countered the marshal, anxious to allay any suspicions as to his motives. 'Now we know the silver has been robbed, the first thing to do is organize a posse,' he hurried on, pushing through the restive crowd. 'Any man wants to join up, get your weapons and meet me in the saloon in fifteen minutes.'

That was enough to disperse the throng.

Thirty minutes later, the new day was nudging over the eastern horizon as Jonas Kelly led the posse out of town in a westerly direction. His first point of call had to be Apache Pass.

Jonas trusted that Curly Ben would have seen fit to disguise the tortuous route he had taken to reach the bolt-hole at Pueblo Bonita. All of the ten men making up the group were town dwellers who appeared to have little capability of reading sign. For that he was grateful. It would make his job of leading them on a fruitless quest in pursuit of the bandits all the more plausible.

It was a brutal shock to all their systems when they eventually came across the bloody arena of the abandoned silver wagon. Especially for Jonas who had emphasized a wish that the guards should not be harmed.

He had not thought to ask the mineworker about their fate. The fact that two graves lay adjacent to the trail told its own story. That had to be the work of Chavez. He had encountered the Mexican's need to assuage his religious conscience before.

After releasing the four remaining horses from their traces, Jonas sent the employee back to the Trujillo Mine to inform the owner of the horrific occurrence. A cursory search of the immediate surroundings brought forth an unexpected result.

'Over here, Marshal,' called out Kansas Pete who had wandered back down the ravine a'ways. He was leading the recently acquired Apaloosa stallion he had purchased with his share of the Chandler reward. 'I think I've found one of the robbers.'

The others quickly hustled over to the spot where the livery hand was peering down behind some rocks.

Gingerly, one by one the rest of the posse peeked over the boulder at the splayed-out body. It was not a pretty sight. Already the coyotes had been hard at work.

But the guy was still recognizable as the Dakota Kid.

Jonas sucked in his breath. The others likewise recoiled at the gruesome remains that had once been a human being. For the storekeeper, Faron Bentley, it was all too much to absorb. The contents of his stomach welled up, spewing forth in an nauseating torrent. The gasping councillor quickly stumbled away to recover.

Luckily for the marshal, nobody had heeded his

stupefied look at seeing the corpse of his confederate. Realizing his mouth was hanging askew, the lawman's craggy features quickly arranged themselves into a suitably deadpan, inscrutable cast.

'It ain't one of our men,' concurred the prospector rubbing his jaw. 'Has to be one of the gang.'

The others nodded in agreement.

'At least the guards got one before they were shot down,' sneered Pete.

Jonas's thinking was striking out in a totally opposite direction.

What had happened here?

Had the Kid been shot down during the hold-up? If so, why was his body found almost a hundred yards from the scene of the confrontation. Nobody else appeared to have noted this disparity. And it appeared to have been deliberately hidden from view. Why? It didn't make any sense.

These and other questions flooded Jonas's pounding head. What ought to have been a simple heist was becoming a baffling mystery.

Then it struck him with the force of one of the Bulldog Maddox's piledrivers.

The gang had had a disagreement following the hold-up. Dakota had come off worst. The Kid's body had been hidden so his mean-eyed face would not be recognized and point the finger at the Clovis Gang.

The true nature of the terminal confrontation was still a mystery. But he had no doubt that all would be revealed in due course. What mattered for now was to go along with the general opinion that the gang was one man down.

'Leave the sneaking rat where he is. Let the critters enjoy a good feast for a change,' ordered the marshal brusquely, 'Now let's ride. We've gotta catch these coyotes afore they leave the state.'

Without further comment he led the way back to the tethered mounts.

For the next three days, Jonas Kelly – assumed US Marshal – led the posse across the southern reaches of Colorado; north, to the blunt upsurge of the La Garita Mountains through which only the brave or down-right foolish ventured. Sane travellers took a detour by way of Salida, or turned back.

Kelly chose the latter option. Then it was south to Chimney Rock where the Navajo tribal lands began, thus precluding any further investigation on pain of having their scalps lifted. Westward to Durango where they learned that no unauthorized silver shipments had come through.

Just like the elusive silver, the posse's alternatives were fast disappearing.

Heading back east, they passed through numerous abandoned settlements where mining was no longer viable. The bleached bones of rotting structures were a haunting reminder of the fate awaiting all such towns once the rich motherlode ran dry.

Late on the evening of the third day, the posse made camp outside one such ghost town. A broken sign informed them they had entered Contention. At least it offered the possibility of cover for the night.

Unsaddling his mount, Jonas couldn't help noting that the posse was becoming restless and edgy. With no sign of the gang, a lugubrious melancholia was setting in. Questions were being raised as to the marshal's plan of campaign. Did he have any notion as to which direction the gang had headed after committing the robbery?

Jonas responded to this slur on his competence by bluntly offering the lead to any other member of the posse who felt he could do better.

Nobody accepted the challenge.

A couple were even beginning to question the need for going on any longer. After all, couldn't the owner of the Trujillo Mine claim the loss on his insurance policy? Jonas dutifully reminded them all that two innocent men had lost their lives. They owed their families a duty to do all that was possible to bring the perpetrators to justice. The brittle retort effectively stifled any further slur as to his capability.

Nevertheless, he was ready to bring the charade to a close.

'Seems to me as if they've given us the slip,' announced the suitably doleful lawdog on the morning of the fourth day. He held up his arms to admit defeat. 'All I can do now is inform the state legislature to post Wanted dodgers in all towns engaged in the refining of silver.' He waited for this declaration to sink in. 'So I propose that we head back to Hashknife.'

Some of the posse members visibly sighed with relief. Others attempted to stifle any sign of cheer that the futile pursuit was being terminated. Kansas Pete alone was for continuing.

He was vigorously overruled by the others.

And so the mournful posse turned east back into Conejos County.

It was mid-afternoon of the following day when the tired riders crested the final rise. The huddle of clapboard buildings that was Hashknife lay before them in the broad hollow. It was a welcome sight.

Entering the outskirts of the small settlement, Jonas couldn't fail to notice a horse tied up to the hitching rail outside the jailhouse. It was a large, black Arab stallion that he didn't recognize as belonging to a local citizen.

Alarm bells immediately rang in his head. His whole body stiffened.

The new lawman – the real marshal had finally arrived.

The guy must be inside the office, waiting. And maybe he had the mayor and leading members of the council in there as back-up. Even now they could be drawing a bead on him. A feeling of *déjà vu* rippled through his taut frame. Nervously he fingered the pistol on his right hip.

With a supreme effort of will he shrugged off the tightness in his guts.

The other members of the posse did not appear to have noticed the marshal's discomfort, anxious as they were to get home, or slake their thirst in the saloon. Jonas offered everybody a perfunctory thank you which was acknowledged with a series of muttered grunts as they split up.

But his mind was focused on the black stallion – and its owner.

FIFTEEN

BROTHERS-IN-ARMS

Jonas paused, his hand on the office door handle. He replayed in his whirling mind the scenario he had created to explain away his deception.

Then he slowly opened the door and entered the gloomy interior. His narrowed eyes, alert to any sign that he was about to be denounced, immediately noticed a lone figure on the far side of the room. The guy was a touch shorter than himself but stockier with broad shoulders. His straight back was to Jonas.

'Can I do something for you, mister?' he asked, injecting a terse bite into the question to conceal his unease.

The man was studying a list of Wanted dodgers pinned up on the noticeboard. As if in slow motion, he swung round on his boot heels. The movement was effortless, that of a man confident of his position.

The two men stared at one another.

Jonas could not make out the other man's features shaded beneath a broad-brimmed black plainsman. It matched the rest of his gear. The marshal squinted hard as he tried to focus on the enigmatic stranger. There was something familiar about the guy's stance; legs placed apart, thumbs hooked into the tooled leather gunbelt with its twin holsters.

It was when the man uttered his first words that the bogus marshal staggered back apace. He clutched at the door jamb for support, eyes bulging wide with disbelief. But there was no denying that voice even though he hadn't heard the familiar cadence for over ten years.

'It's been a long time, little brother.'

Mitch!

A beam of sunlight reflected off the five-pointed sheriff's star pinned to the other man's chest. So his own brother was the real lawman. Jonas Kelly was left speechless. The seismic shock took some getting used to.

'Seems to me like you've gotten a deal of explaining to do,' drawled Mitchell Kelly as he moved over to the stove and poured out a mug of coffee. Stepping up to his brother, the sheriff handed him the steaming brew. 'Drink this and sit down. You look as if you've seen a ghost.' A gruff chortle of laughter seemed to break the spell that had stunned his younger brother into immobility.

'You could say that,' mumbled Jonas, gratefully accepting the mug.

He sat down and sipped at the strong liquid. It was a full five minutes before either man ventured a further comment. Meeting up after all these years, and under these circumstances, took some absorbing. Jonas's mind slipped back through the years to their last meeting. It had not been a happy one. Both men setting off to enlist in the war, but on different sides.

Eventually he put his feelings into words.

'I'm just glad that we never met up.' The remark emerged as a throaty gurgle, the emotive sentiment threatening to overwhelm him. 'During or since the war.'

'There were some close shaves,' added Mitch offering his brother a cigar. Jonas nodded his thanks. Lighting up, he was fully aware that they each operated on different sides of the law. Tendrils of blue smoke twined and swayed in the still air as both men tried to assimilate the unique situation in which they were now embroiled.

But it was the older brother who had the questions to ask. And he knew that the answers would not be to his liking.

'So!' he began with a tight sigh. 'You ready to tell me what this is all about?' Mitch Kelly's tone was flat, his face a stony mask.

Crunch time had arrived.

Jonas had decided to abandon the prepared rationale for explaining his presence in Hashknife. His brother's unexpected arrival had dynamically stymied

143

that course of action. In short he had decided to throw caution to the wind and tell all as it had occurred. Brushing over the failed hold-up at Manzanola Draw, he briefly outlined the aftermath up to and including the fanciful pursuit of the Trujillo silver heist.

Mitch listened carefully, absorbing the erratic sequence of events and interjecting only to clarify certain points.

'So where are Curly Ben and his boys hiding out now?' he finally responded.

'They are waiting for me to quit Hashknife and join them at Pueblo Bonita,' said Jonas. 'It was my intention to take the old Indian trail down into New Mexico. We could have been across the border in three days.' A deep almost regretful sigh emerged from his tight-lipped mouth. Had he done the right thing in telling all this to his brother, a legitimate officer of the law?

Mitch held his gaze with fixed determination.

'So does that mean you have changed your mind?'

Jonas stood up and began pacing the small office. His mind was in a quandary. He reckoned to be a faster draw than his brother. All he needed to do was whip out his pistol and pull the trigger then claim the guy was one of the outlaws. His hand rested on the butt of the Peacemaker.

Mitch remained seated, puffing casually on his cigar. Only the steely glint in his narrowed eyes betrayed a brooding uncertainty. But he knew his brother. There was no way the younger man would

144

draw down on his own kin.

Jonas was in two minds when a lithe figure appeared in the doorway. Both men swivelled their gaze to the portrait of loveliness, her stunning profile starkly framed against the bright background. Hashknife's very own answer to the Mona Lisa.

That did it.

No way could Jonas pull the trigger on his own brother, nor did he want to abandon the new life he had begun to carve out for himself.

Unaware of the chilly atmosphere into which she had broken, Rachel sauntered into the office.

'Yet another new face. You are a popular man, Jonas,' she observed with a wry smile.

'Erm!' stammered the outlaw. 'This is my brother Mitch. He's been sent over from Denver to—'

The elder Kelly stood up and quickly interposed, 'I'm the new marshal. My brother here came ahead to look after things until I had completed some unfinished business at head office.' Mitch held his brother's wavering eye. 'He's going to be my deputy, aren't you, Brother?'

For the briefest of moments, a flicker of indecision showed in the square-jawed demeanour of the outlaw, Jim Kane. But the startled yet radiantly gladdened face of Rachel Summers dissipated any loyalty he had felt towards Curly Ben Clovis.

'That's right,' he averred, 'Mitch has brought news that the gang who robbed the Trujillo silver wagon are holed up nearby. We were just about to set off after them when you turned up.'

'There's no time to form a new posse,' cut in Mitch Kelly, reaching for a Winchester rifle. 'Jonas and I reckon we can surprise the gang in their hideout on Pueblo Bonita, but we'll need to set off right away to stop them escaping over the state line.'

'It's going to need more than two of you to stop that bunch of killers,' emphasized Rachel likewise reaching for one of the remaining carbines.

'You can't come,' blurted out a distraught Jonas Kelly. 'It far to dangerous for a—'

'—For a woman?' butted in the feisty girl. 'Let me tell you, Jonas Kelly, that I've been shooting rabbits since I was a child. Even Windy Rivers says I'm the best shot with a long gun in the county.'

'But these are desperate criminals, Miss Summers,' Mitch emphasized in support of his brother's objection. 'They wouldn't hesitate to shoot a woman.' He could see that there was more than mere regard for her safety in the way his brother looked at the girl.

'I have Windy outside; he'll back me up, I'm certain,' countered Rachel with fiery vigour. 'And four of us would ensure that the gang don't escape.'

Haughtily she waited for their reaction. Hands firmly planted on hips, Rachel silently challenged the two lawmen to overrule her resolve to accompany them.

Jonas shrugged.

'It's up to you, Brother,' he sighed, 'you're the sheriff.'

'OK, you're in,' he announced. 'But as elected officers of the law, we make the decisions. And you do as you're told. Agreed?'

'Agreed.'

SIXTEEN

PUEBLO BONITA

After Rachel had gone outside to impart the news to Windy Rivers that he was joining a new posse, Mitch quickly assured his brother that when this was over, he would endeavour to bury Jim Kane along with his murky past.

'The state governor owes me a few favours.' He winked, tapping his nose in a gesture of wily intrigue. 'I'll get him to grant you a pardon. Wipe out all your previous . . . indiscretions. He won't be able to say no when I convince him that you'll be working for me.'

Jonas thanked him, but he was less optimistic than his brother. There had been a heap of so-called indiscretions over the years. It would have to be a very obliging governor who could overlook such crimes. Did one exist? Not in his book. Mitch was pissing into the wind even to consider the notion. But he just smiled amiably whilst checking his weapons.

Within a half-hour, the small group of riders were taking a back trail out of Hashknife to avoid the prying eyes of Elmer Flockhart and his cronies. This was no time to explain the sudden change of legal representation in the town. That could come when the robbers had been dealt with.

As Jonas was more familiar with the local terrain, Mitch allowed him to take the lead. Windy Rivers fell in at the rear. Two large appealing green eyes had effectually dissolved any qualms he might have entertained regarding the imminent showdown.

Riding beside his brother, Jonas conveyed the opinion that the gang would not have ventured up to the abandoned ruins of the pueblo itself on the top of the broad mesa.

The heavily laden mules would have found it impossible to climb the steep narrow track which meant the silver would have to be manhandled. Only Bulldog Maddox was capable of such a Herculean task. And even he would have balked at the idea, then having to cart it all down again after a few days. And Clovis would not want to be separated from the lucre for a minute.

'He'll find a secluded hollow among the rocks at the foot of the mesa,' he opined. 'So we will need to be extra vigilant as we get near.'

'How d'you figure we should approach the place?' Mitch Kelly was cognizant of his brother's sharp mind. And, as an ex-member of the gang, he was acutely aware of the younger man's valuable knowledge regarding the manner of Curly Ben's warped thought processes.

149

'We leave the horses down at the base of Pueblo Bonita,' Jonas stressed, 'then sneak up through the boulder-field on foot. There's plenty of cover. But that goes for the gang as well. They'll be well dug in.' He lodged a cautionary eye on to his brother. 'Don't underestimate Ben Clovis. The guy's a tough cookie, and smart with it. And he's got two hard-bitten desperadoes to back him up to the hilt.'

The towering monolith was now clearly in view some two miles to the east just off the main trail. Fractured turrets of naked orange sandstone soared skyward that not even a mountain goat could climb.

Jonas signalled a stop. Removing a pair of binoculars from his saddle-bag, he carefully swept the near horizon trying to pick out any trace of movement among the clutter of rocks. The steady movement back and forth was suddenly brought to an abrupt halt.

'They're up there all right,' he asserted firmly. His finger pointed to the base of the surging mesa as he handed the binoculars to Mitch. 'This is where we leave the mounts.' Stepping down, they ground hitched them behind a screen of blooming yucca. 'Check your hardware and follow me,' Jonas ordered, offering Rachel an assured smile. This was not like hunting rabbits.

Mitch offered his brother a brief nod of approval as they set off hunching low to preclude any chance of being spotted.

Weaving in and out between loose rocks and the stands of cholla cactus, spiny thorns from stunted arms of mesquite endeavoured to slow their progress. Splashes of yellow and orange from bunched clusters of prickly pear helped relieve the monotonous dun shade of the arid landscape.

Only the need to get as close to the mesa as possible without raising the alarm mattered. As they drew closer, Mitch hissed for them to rest in the cover of some isolated juniper bushes.

'We need to spread out,' he advised. 'Sticking together like this, they'll spot us much more easily. You go round to the left,' he told Windy Rivers.

Turning to face Rachel, he addressed her in a deliberate manner. For his brother's sake, the last thing he wanted was to place her in any danger, but neither did he want the peppery young woman to feel she was being protected.

'Your prowess with a long gun will suit us best up in those rocks.'

He jabbed a finger towards a ledge some fifty feet above their present position jutting out from a low butte known as Goblin's Roost. It offered a panoramic view of Pueblo Bonita from a much more elevated site. He waited, flinty-eyed, for her to demur, but she merely nodded in agreement.

'Jonas and I will make a frontal assault, that all right with you, Brother?'

The younger man recognized that Mitch had more experience of dealing with holed-up desperadoes. Until this moment, Jim Kane, outlaw, had always been on the receiving end of legal confrontations, shooting his way out of critical situations when cornered. He

151

had no doubts of Mitch Kelly's capacity to smoke the varmints out.

But he also knew that Curly Ben Clovis would be no pushover. The gang boss would fight tooth and nail to escape a hangman's rope. Both of the men that he had left would be posted in strategic positions to warn of any impending assault on their position.

It came sooner than expected.

The sharp crack from a Springfield rifle ripped apart the silence. Windy Rivers had been a mite careless in edging up the shallow gradient. All it took was a momentary exposure for the eagle-eye of Ben Clovis to cut him down. And the grating yelp of pain was enough to inform the others that their surprise assault had been thwarted.

Both sides now opened up. The air was soon fizzing with the crackle of hot lead. Gunsmoke drifted across the harsh terrain.

Mitch Kelly figured to take advantage of the confusion by hustling up the gently shelving slope thus getting in closer to their quarry. Bending low, six-gun clutched tightly in his right hand, he scuttled between the limited cover offered by the boulder field.

Well-aimed bullets followed his progress, whining and ricochetting off the rocks. None found its mark. Only when the lawman was forced to hunker down and reload his .45 did the precarious nature of his position become apparent.

Bulldog Maddox quickly saw the chance of finishing off the helpless lawman. Once again, the outlaw proved his ability to step lively when the occasion demanded. And this was just such a moment. Scurrying across the open ground separating the two protagonists, he drew down on Mitch's squatting body.

An evil grimace, crooked and menacing, accompanied the guttural rasp of triumph as he cut loose.

'That's another one less to worry about, boss,' he snarled, despatching a couple of slugs into the defenceless body. Mitch Kelly keeled over, blood spurting from his punctured body.

But at that very same moment, a resonant boom snapped back off the nearby rocky tower of the mesa. A puff of smoke issued from a crevice high up on a ledge of rock some hundred yards distant.

Rachel Summers smiled, her eyes squinting along the length of the Winchester. She accorded herself a brief nod of approval. Dead centre and not bad for a mere rabbit shooter. That big lumbering ox would not be getting up from that in a hurry. Angry shots akin to droning hornets bombarded the ledge in retaliation. But Rachel was too well concealed. Dislocated fragments of rock whirled impotently above her head.

When Jonas saw his brother go down, even the felling of Bulldog Maddox was no compensation. Dejectedly, his head slumped on to his chest. After all these years, to be taken away so suddenly. It was more than a person should have to bear. Tears filled his eyes. He slumped down behind a boulder, his innards clenching and twisting until the pain brought him round.

That was when a fresh resolve filled the aching void in his heart; an iron determination to avenge the brutal removal of his closest kin. The ache in his stomach was a catharsis, a sign urging him onward to fulfil the task of eradicating the Clovis Gang from civilization.

And there was a way of turning this apparent disaster to his distinct advantage. Quickly he signalled to Rachel to remain where she was as he gingerly edged over towards his right. After ten minutes, he found what he was seeking. A narrow gully snaked upwards pursuing a tortuous route that effectively concealed him from the enemy.

For that is what they now were.

The enemy!

Loose gravel and stones underfoot needed care. Not only to avoid injury, but to ensure that those above were not given advance warning of his approach.

Emerging from the confines of the narrow fissure, Jonas checked his revolver. Thumb lightly resting on the gnurled spiggot of the hammer, he crept out on to the shelf adjacent to the main track that led up to the ruins of the pueblo itself. Immediately in front was the start of the old Indian trail with the four mules hobbled together in line.

And over to his left crouched the gang leader, peering from between a cluster of rocks. Jonas's face cracked in a lurid smile. Clovis was totally unaware that he had been duped. And, as expected, his back was facing the new deputy marshal.

Tense and edgy, Clovis still figured that he was in control. He had removed his hat so as not to offer an obvious target. The mass of curly black hair hung lank and greasy in the static air.

With consummate regard to ensuring a silent approach, Jonas picked his way across the flat expanse avoiding loose dry twigs and rocks, the Peacemaker aimed at the outlaw's broad back.

Sucking in a deep breath, he thumbed back the revolver's hammer to full cock. The distinctive sound saw the exposed back visibly stiffen.

'It's the end of the line, Ben,' affirmed Jonas tersely. 'Best to throw down your rifle and give yourself up.'

'Ugh!' growled Clovis, instantly recognizing the voice of his erstwhile lieutenant. 'So the Kid was right after all,' His voice was harsh and discordant. 'You are a Judas. A skulkin' backshooter who's betrayed his pards. I shoulda listened to the sonofabitch from the start, even though he did wear the same coat.'

'What are you talking about?' queried Jason.

'The bastard only tried to steal the silver for himself.' Clovis emitted a mirthless guffaw. 'I showed him that nobody gets one over on Curly Ben. Especially some no-account kid from the wrong side of the tracks.'

Clovis slowly swung round to face his old confederate, right hand poised above the butt of his .45.

'Keep them hands high where I can see them,' hissed Jonas, jabbing his pistol forward, 'One false move and I'll drill you without a second's thought.'

Muttering a lurid curse, Clovis slowly, but reluctantly, obeyed.

'So why did you become a turncoat, Jim? Was it that

bit of skirt you was a-makin' eyes at? Or maybe like Dakota, you also have designs on keepin' the silver all for yourself?'

'Respect, Ben,' stressed Jonas. 'Something I'd never get sticking with the likes of you. And I don't just mean by being a fast gun with an itchy trigger finger. For the first time in my life, folks looked up to me, raised their hats when I walked down the street. And yeah, Rachel has played a part, a big part. But the main reason was meeting up with my brother again.'

Clovis angled a crooked frown at him.

'And my real name is Jonas Kelly, not Jim Kane. Mitch had agreed to get me a pardon from the state governor if I helped bring you in.'

'Not *the* Mitchell Kelly?' gaped Clovis. 'The hell-raisin' starpacker from Denver who brought in the Branson Gang singled-handed?'

'One and the same,' preened Jonas, proud of his brother's infamous reputation in lawless circles.

'I am impressed, Jim, or should I say Jonas?' smirked Clovis.

But a grey cast had settled over Jonas Kelly's granite features. His next words were full of harsh invective.

'But now he's lying dead down there. So all that has gone down the Swanee. But I'm gonna make sure you hang for his murder.'

'I don't think so, mister.' The gang leader's gaze shifted to a point beyond the deputy's right shoulder. 'Take him out now.'

Jonas coughed out a brittle laugh. 'Think I'd be stupid enough to fall for that old chestnut?' he rapped out, keeping his gun hand steady and unwavering.

'Eet ees no old chestnut as you say, *amigo*.' The Mexican hawked a gob of spittle into the sand. 'But *compadres* do not betray each other.'

'Chavez!'

He'd forgotten all about the little greaser. Now he was stuck between the devil and the deep blue sea. With no place to swim.

'Why you go against old buddies?' The lilting cadence sounded forlorn, almost disappointed. 'You let me down, Jeem. For that I have to keel you.' Then on a brighter note he added, 'But for you, a good burial, *sí*?'

For what seemed like an hour, in fact less than five seconds, a heavy silence shrouded the grim scene. It was Clovis who broke it knowing this was his final chance to square things.

'Take him out, Chavez!' he hissed.

That was when a loud crack split the ether.

Seconds later, there was a metallic clatter as the Bowie knife struck a rock immediately followed by the muted thud of a falling body.

Clovis flung himself to the left, clawing at the smokepole on his hip. Two shots rang out simultaneously.

Ten minutes later, Rachel Summers stumbled up on to the rocky shelf. She gasped at the sight that met her staring eyes. The Mexican had half his head missing, the remainder was scattered over the surrounding rocks. Her finely contoured face blanched as she realized that the grisly picture was her doing. To her left

157

Jonas Kelly was standing over the body of the man in black whom she had last seen in the marshal's office. Although now his clothes were stained a violent shade of crimson.

Wobbly legs somehow propelled her across the open tract. It was her shadow that alerted Jonas to the alien presence behind him. Unthinking, he swung in a single fluid movement. The arcing Peacemaker racked back, was barely a half-second from being discharged. In the nick of time he caught sight of the girl. An audible sigh of relief escaped from his gaping mouth on realizing what could have happened.

Gently she took his hand and led him away from the gruesome scene of carnage. A plaintive braying from the tethered mules echoed the emotive feelings of those who had survived the brutal exchange of fire. The creatures were restive, anxious to be gone. But that would have to wait. The silver was going nowhere. Cranford Jagger could arrange for it to be banked.

But first there were bodies that needed attending to.

Windy Rivers was clearly in view splayed over a boulder where he'd fallen. Together, they reverently carried the old bronc buster down the rough slope. Rachel tried to remain stoic, but couldn't keep the tears from her eyes. After wrapping him in a sleeping tarp, they secured him over the saddle of his horse and went in search of Mitchell Kelly.

'Last I saw of him was when that hulking brute gunned him down.' Rachel peered towards a clump of ocotillo, the plant's fiery red blossoms standing proud like a blood stain. 'Then he disappeared.'

It was the finality of the flat almost glacial way in which she said it that conjured up the realization that Mitchell Kelly was dead.

Rachel led the way up the rising slope of scrub and rocky detritus to where Mitch was lying. As they drew nearer, Jonas drew in a sharp intake of breath. Was that a slight movement he detected? He screwed up his eyes against the sun's harsh glare. There it was again – his brother was still alive, however tenuously.

He hurried across the intervening few yards and bent down, cradling the injured man's head in his arms. Rachel passed a water bottle over and he dribbled a few drops into the parched mouth.

Luckily, the wounds were not fatal even though he was bleeding badly. One bullet had removed half his ear while the the other had gouged a rut in his rib cage.

Without thought or embarrassment, Rachel hitched up her leather riding skirt and ripped a couple of strips from her petticoat. She then set about staunching the leakage of blood with a bandage wrapped tightly around his head.

'He needs a doctor,' she stated with steadfast conviction, 'and quickly!'

Mitch groaned as they lifted him on to his feet. But at least he had regained consciousness. Working together, they somehow managed to get him down to his horse unscathed.

The ride back to Hashknife was unavoidably slow under the circumstances.

Not until they were halfway to town did Mitch Kelly find the strength to utter his first words. His brother's taut features lit up with obvious relief. The wheezing remark was aimed at Rachel, and punctuated by a series of gasping intakes.

'You make sure . . . to keep a close eye on this fella . . . while I'm recuperating.' His features were ashen and caked in dried blood. But there was a gleam in his eye that was like pure nectar to Jonas. 'He'll have to . . . stand in for me . . . until I can make the job . . . official.'

Rachel laughed.

'He'll be sick of the sight of me inside a week.'

Jonas scratched his head in playful consideration.

'Maybe I will in five years when you're nagging me to mend that garden fence and grease the water pump,' he muttered, offering his brother a half smile accompanied by a crafty wink. 'Until then, I'll cope.'